Not The Fighting Kind

Not That Kind Of Dandy 1

Will Soulsby-McCreath

ISBN: 978-1-7399525-9-4 (eBook),
978-1-7399525-8-7 (paperback)

First Edition

WillSoulsbyMcCreath.com

For those of us who are, always, too much.

Content Warning:

Moderate depictions of violence and injury, some implied dubious consent, scenes of consensual intimacy.

For more detailed content warnings please visit WillSoulsbyMcCreath.com

A quick note about pronouns:

If you are unfamiliar with neo-pronouns, they do appear in this novel. In particular you'll come across the singular they, as well as others like ey, eir, em and xe, xyr, xem.

Also By Will Soulsby-McCreath

The Guardian Cadet Series
Merry Arlan: Breaking The Curse
Merry Arlan: Finding The Heir
Kitty Hughes: An Unexpected Meeting (short
story)

Welcome To Humanity

Inter-Planetary Alliance Novels
Unlicensed Delivery

Not That Kind Of Dandy
Not The Fighting Kind
Not The Fainting Kind
Not That Kind Of Dandy Omnibus

Not The Fighting Kind

Not That Kind Of Dandy

1

Will Soulsby-McCreath

1

Many Things, But Not A Fool

The swirl of a ball was a delicate thing. Gowns twirled in a kaleidoscope of colours and details, reflecting light where they shone with gems, trailing fabric across the floor and in swooshes of wrist straps and sleeves. The stiff blocks of gentlemen's clothes like the lines in a stained glass window.

Nat had been enthralled with the balance of it all for longer than they could remember. Sneaking down from their room to investigate, to the extent that their father had despaired and begun locking their bedroom door on hosting nights.

That was how Nat usually got into trouble. Caught doing something they shouldn't. Drawn in by something beautiful.

That had to be what had Nat's head pounding with pain. Drawn in by something. Maybe a challenge. Maybe a swirling pretty thing. But no...

A hard floor pressed against their back. A soft swooshing sound filtered into focus. Where in the world were they?

Oh.

Right.

The ship.

Nat held in a groan as they pushed into a sitting position. Everything hurt. And they didn't even have the joy of an event's gossip to carry them through the experience.

But something still wasn't right. A windowless, dark room with the gentle rattle of metal on metal buzzing in the space. A naval bunk this was not.

The twenty-odd other people they had shared the bunk with were a noisy bunch. Their snoring, shuffling, whispering was notably absent here. And the lantern hung by the door for emergencies that had assaulted Nat's eyes for many a night had either been extinguished or it, similarly, was not present.

More relevant even, was the lack of bunk, the lack of shitty straw mattress and scratchy threadbare blanket. It wasn't much of a bed. Nevertheless, this was even less of one. Never would Nat have thought they would seek comfort from the naval bunk. Every time it came to mind, Nat wanted to cry. Not that one cried in public, let alone on a naval ship.

Rubbing their eyes as if it might clear the darkness, pain tugged at their attention. Their arms hurt. When did they not these days? But this was different somehow. And Nat would really like to be able to quantify the how and the why but without sight that didn't seem like a possibility.

They shifted in an attempt to better make out the room. If this was some kind of joke by Rodgerson, Nat was going to scream. He was the type to think it was funny to shove Nat into a dark cupboard somewhere and leave them there to get reprimanded by the Rear-Admiral for being late to deck. Again. It wasn't like Nat needed help with that.

Pushing past the indignity of it – if they couldn't see, then nobody else could see them – Nat crawled carefully forward. Their knees called for attention. Another mystery pain to categorise at some point.

The lack of memory concerned them more. A head injury perhaps? Or poison. Unlikely but so was waking up in a pitch dark room one hadn't fallen asleep in.

They ran their hands over the floor: wooden, worn. Where was the edge of the room? Ideally a door Nat could escape through. The blunt edge of an iron bar bit into Nat's probing fingers.

They flinched back and silently cursed themself for it. Returning, more carefully, to the bars, Nat traced them. Flat iron, criss-crossed into squares large enough for Nat to get both hands through but not large enough for any other portion of their body.

At least they had found the source of the rattling metal noise.

Nat sank back on their feet, ignoring the way it would probably leave marks on their trousers. Screw passing inspection at this point. This was a cell.

How had this come to pass?

Blurry, faded images of a rainstorm came to mind. The Rear-Admiral's voice booming, calling everyone to man their positions. Nat's bunkmates had surged to their feet, pulling on some semblance of uniform and grabbing for swords Nat had never before seen them use.

The man who slept below Nat, the one with the nasal whistle that kept Nat up all night, yanked Nat down by a leg. Their knee slammed against the ground with a thunk that carried over both the shouting and the raging storm outside.

At least that explained the knee pain.

"Get dressed," he demanded. "And man your fucking post!" Nobody said naval boys had any manners.

Nat rubbed their face again. What had happened after that? Why had they needed to man posts? And why with swords? Nat had never used a sword in their life.

There was no point dwelling on the events of the previous night. Maybe Nat would be able to remember the cause of the rest of their pain, maybe they wouldn't. It wouldn't do them any good either way. They were in a cell of some sort, presumably captured by whoever had boarded the ship the previous night.

That could be better. But it left Nat with a potential course of action and that was all they really needed. Find a way out.

Was anyone else here too?

Nat sucked in a deep breath and held it, listening intently for the sound of breath over the quiet whoosh of the sea. Before they could begin to count, a light bloomed in the doorway to their left.

The room itself was long and slim. Nat inhabited the furthest cell from the doorway. A square space with two solid wooden walls and two sets of cell bars. Nat had found their way toward the one with the door, opposite which sat more of that bland wooden walling across a narrow corridor, no wider than the doorway itself.

"Good," the lantern-holder said, voice deep and accented — Kovian if Nat was guessing. "You're awake. Captain will be glad to hear it."

The illumination, still too bright to really make out the pirate beyond broad shoulders, clarified that Nat was not, in fact, completely alone in the row of cells. Three other members of *The Valliant's* crew filled the other three cells in the room. And by what Nat knew of their families, someone on *The Valiant* had sold them out. How else would the pirates have ended up with four prisoners from upper class, well-to-do families?

This was a ransom mission.

The pirate approached the first cells, staring down at Lord Felitabby. His strawberry blonde hair – more blonde than strawberry – hung halfway out of his usual ponytail, lending him a dishevelled look only furthered by the looseness of his cravat knot.

Did he get to go by Lord on this ship? Or was it replaced with his naval title? *The Valliant*'s crew mostly referred to him by his surname, same as Rodgerson. But what would be the appropriate thing to call him here?

Nat wanted to rub their face and groan. Ever the dandy, they could apparently be on a pirate ship, in a cell on a pirate ship, and still be considering appropriate manners of address.

"Tell me your name," the pirate demanded.

Felitabby squared up with the pirate through the cell bars. He sneered. "I won't tell a pirate anything."

The pirate shrugged, seemingly unfazed. He moved on to Mr Awthorn's cell door.

Awthorn trembled, lay uncomfortably against the back wall, one hand grasped to his side. Blood darkened the blue and white of his naval uniform, painted his hands, stained the wood around him.

The pirate crouched, lantern dipping with him, creating strange patterns on the wall that filled Nat's head with an awkward combination of ball-like refractions and images of sea monsters. "I can offer you bandages and even our ship surgeon if you tell me who you are."

"M-Mr Jym Awthorn."

"Son of...?"

"Jym Awthorn."

That was it then. Nat's inclination had been correct. This was a ransom attempt.

Fuck.

The pirate shifted, revealing a bag slung across his body. He pulled medical supplies from it and pushed them through the bars toward Awthorn, his whole arm slipping between the iron bands to leave them as close to the injured Awthorn as possible. "I will bring the surgeon down later."

He stood and shifted to Viscount Archin in the cell next to Nat. Nat had always felt a little sorry for Archin. The fifth son, he had no hope of inheriting anything, leaving his options as military prowess or rakery, and, poor Nial had never had the time to develop social capability before shipping out even if he was pretty enough with his long eyelashes and easily flushed skin.

His unblemished face twisted into something akin to pride. Foolish youth, Nat supposed. Men like Nial Archin idolised types like Rodgerson and Felitabby.

"Tell me who you are," the pirate demanded.

"I am a proud naval officer."

Silence sat heavy over the room, the rustling of Awthorn attempting to bandage his wounds and the swoosh of the sea the only noises.

"I..." Archin hedged. "I don't have much family to speak of."

The pirate let out a little, disappointed laugh. "I should warn you, all of you, that if you are not of use to us the Captain may not see fit to keep you around."

One last glance at Felitabby and Archin cracked, the words falling out of his mouth like water out of a bucket. "Archin, sir. I am the fifth Archin son. My father is Count Archin of the Groves."

Finally the pirate stood, with his swinging lantern, directly in front of Nat's cells. The soft orange glow lending him an ethereal quality, painting him entirely in that orange light: hair, skin, even his eyes.

Nat pushed to their feet, sauntered the few steps to the bars and leaned against them, one arm —the uninjured one— raised above their head to create the contrapposto of the Classical Elikkae statues. They slipped easily into their dandified smile, their eyes raking up and down the pirate's form. Performative, but he didn't need to know that.

His shirt didn't fit— not by Nat's standards at least. He fit in it, sure, but that was not the same thing. It was, to his credit, neatly tucked into his black trousers, which in turn were tucked into brown leather boots. Off-white, black, and brown... it was definitely a combination.

Nat was, however, willing to forgive a little for the clean and well defined musculature of the man in question, as well as his strong jaw and shining blonde hair that lay in an artful scruff across his head.

The pirate mimicked Nat's once over. He raised an eyebrow, eyes flicking to around Nat's temple. "Quite the bruises you've got there."

"Didn't you hear?" Nat's dandy tone was second nature at this point, easy to use and thick as treacle. "Purple and green are all the rage this year in Sirap, and everybody knows Sirap makes the fashions."

The pirate blinked, head flinching back for just an instant. "And what family member of yours has taken you to Sirap?"

Nat laughed, tilting their chin up to expose their throat, even as their heart thundered against their sternum. This was a more dangerous game than any Nat had played before. "Silly pirate, you don't need to go to Sirap to hear about the fashions. That's what magazines are for."

"Fucking dandy," Felitabby snarled.

The animosity didn't matter. Nat didn't care. Or at least couldn't devote any time to that stab of rejection. They had a role to play here, as surely as they did at home.

The pirate didn't agree. He turned his head toward Felitabby. "Do you have something to add to this conversation? Has your tongue loosened?"

"That," Felitabby spat. "Is Liege—"

"Do you really want to start tattling here, My Lord?" Nat interrupted, voice light, falsified joviality. They knew far more about Felitabby's household and income than he knew about theirs. And Nat was almost certain Felitabby couldn't rattle off Nat's family's address. He had never paid them that kind of attention.

Felitabby's mouth clicked shut. Apparently he was smart enough to figure out what Nat meant by that particular comment. They wouldn't have given Thomin the credit.

"So," the pirate refocused on Nat. "Who are you? And for that matter, since you clearly know, who is he?"

"Aw, Peaches," they teased gently, touching a finger to the pirate's crooked nose, ignoring the way even that little motion sent a burning ache up their arm. "You don't get to just ask a *dandy* something, you have to make an offering first."

Again the pirate raised an eyebrow. "Should I remind you again that our Captain does not hold love for people who waste her time and resources?"

Nat shrugged delicately, the motion pulling at the aching muscles they'd already put to overwork by their contrapposto position. "Perhaps she should ask me herself, then."

"I speak for her."

"Then you should know what she might offer."

"Our Captain doesn't offer. She takes."

Nat let out a delicate sigh, pressing their teeth against their tongue at the quiet muttering from their fellow prisoners. This was going to be difficult enough without allowing themself to care about that particular brand of hostility. What could those three do to Nat in these cells anyway? Better to focus on the immediate threat.

"You do not seem afraid of being hurt."

"Let's be honest here, Peaches. If you want to hurt me, you will."

"But you can do things to alleviate the risk."

"No." Nat shook their head, eyes landing on the pirate's scuffed boots. "That's just what people like to tell you. To convince you that their choice is your fault. Ultimately, you have decided already whether you are willing to hurt me or not. My own actions have little to no say in the matter. Why scrabble for the desperate attempt to prevent a pain that will come either way? Why delay what could happen now?" They met his eyes, the same colour as the lantern light and lowered their voice to a whisper. "If you want to kill me, pirate, you might as well get it over with and use it to instil fear in the others."

"You are not afraid?"

"Now, I didn't say that." Nat let out that practised, dandified laugh again. "I'm in a cell on a pirate ship with three supposed allies who hate my guts. Only a fool would be unafraid. And I may be many things, pirate, but I am not a fool."

"Aleksei."

"Excuse me?"

"My name is Aleksei. Aleksei Fyodorovich Zima."

"Nat."

"No surname?"

"Not one I will own at this time, Mr Zima."

"Aleksei," the pirate corrected. He passed another set of medical supplies and a clean, if less than white shirt through the bars into Nat's hands.

Nat's smile shifted to something a little more real, the kind of smile they usually reserved for their younger sister. "Aleksei," they echoed.

2
Less Fearsome Pirate, More Unkempt Ruffian

Nat did not relish having to remove their shirt in the relative public of the cells. They had turned their back to the naval gentlemen, still illuminated by the light Aleksei had left hooked in the doorway, but it hardly counted as private.

But they needed to clean and bandage their injuries and they wanted a shirt that hadn't apparently been torn to pieces if they could have one. So they turned their back to the room and set to unbuttoning their waistcoat.

"Where are we?" Archin asked, his whisper ringing out in the silence.

"Who knows," Felitabby responded.

"We are, quite obviously, on a pirate ship," Nat interjected, no patience for the stupidity being presented at their back. They tipped the small bottle onto a clean cloth, clear liquid spilling out and filling the room with the sharp tang of alcohol.

"And how would you know, dandy?" Felitabby snapped, saying the word dandy as if it were an insult, like it wasn't the title Nat had claimed for themself.

Nat ignored him, pressing the wet rag to the bloodied skin of their arm. Their breath hissed between their teeth. Rivulets of diluted red ran down their skin, dripping onto the floor and seeping into their already dirty uniform trousers. Pink was a nice colour, right?

"How do we get out?" Archin asked.

"If would have been better if you hadn't told them who you were!"

Nat huffed out an irritated breath. "They're going to ransom us. Don't you two know anything about pirates?"

"Ransom us?" Archin asked. "Doesn't that only happen to girls?"

"Obviously not." The words cut off with another hiss of pain. Nat closed their eyes as they held the rag in place. Cold steams of alcohol dragged against their skin. They wanted to cry but this was not an appropriate time or place for such a luxury.

"What do you want to do?" Archin asked.

Nat risked a quick glance over their shoulder to find Archin fully turned toward Felitabby. They shook their head. Those two could try to plot their daring escape if they so wanted, Nat would just focus on keeping themself alive for the time being. If this wound got infected, they would very quickly not have to worry about pirates, ransoms, and stupid naval men, instead entirely consumed by dying from a painful illness.

"They're pretty ruthless." Awthorn's voice came out strained, immediately followed by panting breaths.

"Hey, don't strain yourself," Archin insisted.

"You saw what they did to the dandy," Awthorn insisted. "And they didn't even fight like I did."

Nat continued pressing the cleaning rag to their injuries. As much as they hurt, still hurt, and as much as blood coated Nat's arm, it seemed relatively shallow. At least it wouldn't need stitches. Probably.

They wrapped the clean bandages around it before finally pulling on the new shirt, followed by their grubby waistcoat and cravat.

Sure, this was a pirate ship and Nat was a prisoner aboard it, but there was no reason not to dress properly.

$\mathcal{T}$wo days of languishing in the cells — if the breakfast-like meals and dinner-like meals were anything to gage by — and Nat was almost ready to start plotting with Archin and Felitabby.

The ship's surgeon had appeared to treat Mr Awthorn semi-regularly. His wound was getting worse. No surprise there. Stab wounds were always bad and his had punctured something vital. A sickly pallor coated his face; his harsh, rasping breaths filled the silence of the cells. Nobody, not even Felitabby was willing to speak over it.

After the third breakfast-like meal — Nat wanted to label it oatmeal but it almost had the consistency of very wet rice so they weren't quite sure — had been cleared away, a trio of pirates entered the room. Nat almost couldn't bear to look at them for their attire. Mismatched and ill-fitting pieces of clothing in such a state of disrepair that they almost might as well have not worn anything at all.

The one who unlocked Nat's cell and grabbed them by their uninjured arm had a gaping hole in xyr shirt's elbow, revealing yet more of xyr deep brown skin than the untied shirt collar. How old was that shirt?

The bright sunlight stabbed into Nat's eyes as they stumbled out onto the deck. By the time they had adjusted enough to the light to be able to see at all, they had been tugged up a set of steps to the front of the ship where the Captain stood — if the huge hat resting atop her head was anything to go by. Something about that hat tugged at Nat's memory but they gave it no attention as the woman began to speak. "Navy brats never were good for much," she muttered to Aleksei who stood at her right shoulder. She examined Nat. "Go on then," she invited. "What can you offer?"

Offer? An interesting concept. To request offerings from prisoners. Particularly after Nat had requested the same thing from Aleksei mere days ago. Had he reported it back? Or was this just how the Captain ran things? Four extra mouths to feed with the theory but not promise of ransom payment... She wanted use out of them while they were here. But could it be that simple? Or was the plan to stick four so-called naval brats in ship positions in the hope it might loosen some tongues and surnames?

"I can sew," Nat blurted. Oh. Wonderful. Facing down a pirate captain and they offered sewing!

"Sew?" she echoed, cocking a brow, one hand coming to rest on the hilt of one of the swords strapped to her belt.

"Yes." Nat doubled down. They had never liked being teased like that. Or threatened for that matter. "Embroider, technically, but a stitch is a stitch either way."

"And you think that's useful?"

Nat shifted to mirror her stance as best they could with someone's hand still wrapped around their arm. One hip pushed to one side, hand resting on it. "Are you poorly sighted, Peaches?"

The other eyebrow crawled up to join the first. "Excuse me?"

"Because that's the only possible reason I can imagine for such an obliviousness to the state of dress of your crew."

The Captain folded her arms.

Maybe that was a good sign. At least she wasn't quite so poised to draw her swords anymore.

"Oh, Peaches," Nat gasped. "*Please* tell me you see what I see. They're in disarray. Their clothes scream less fearsome pirate and more..." The paused, eyes pointedly raking over Aleksei. "Unkempt ruffian."

"Ruffian?"

Nat grabbed at the hollowed out elbow of their guard's shirt. "This." They shook it. "Does not create a fearsome image. You look tired and a mess. If you want to create an aura of intimidation, you have to create the *image*."

"You want to mend our clothing?" Aleksei asked, each word more carefully pronounced, like he couldn't quite believe he was saying any of them.

"I'm saying, stitching skills can only ever be useful and I can quite literally see where you need it."

"Fine," the Captain snapped. "Jay, find this one a spot and bring them the clothes that need mending. We shall see how they handle the task."

Nat turned to their guard, Jay, and smiled. "Apologies, grabbing your shirt was a tad forward of me when we weren't even introduced."

Jay tugged Nat over to the edge of the main deck, where a series of barrels had been propped and tied into place. "Do you always talk like that?" Xyr voice had a hint of an accent that had clearly mellowed over years of ship life.

"Like what?"

"Fancy."

Nat let out their practised, dandy laugh. "How else would I address the world?"

"Doesn't it get tiresome?"

"Not even a little." Nat had always been a dandy, even before they knew what a dandy was. The ability to portray oneself to one's own full advantage was something Nat had excelled at from childhood. And, when they had entered society, it had been so easy to slot into the dandy persona, to make dandy friends, to fulfil the role of a dandy. Now it was second nature, even in times of stress, Nat pulled their dandy persona around themself like a comforting blanket.

"I don't think I could do it."

Nat shrugged. "I didn't ask you to."

"You don't think everyone should talk like that?"

"Of course not. We all have our own strengths. We have to work with them, not against them."

Jay glanced over to the Captain, shook xyr head, and dashed off to grab the clothes.

3
That All You Got, Sunflower?

ay had let Nat stitch shirts in peace for the whole remainder of that first day, escorting them back to the cell as the sun dipped below the horizon.

To Nat's surprise, Jay appeared in the cells the next morning also. Although xe had subsequently requested Aleksei take over guarding Nat in that same spot by the barrels.

Even this early on in the pile, which seemed somehow to be growing rather than shrinking, it was clear that it would be far easier to relegate the entire pile to cleaning supplies and just buy new. Somehow, Nat didn't think the captain would appreciate them sharing that particular opinion with her.

Across the deck, Felitabby half-heartedly swiped a mop back and forth. His own guard, a humongous man who resembled nothing so much as a bear, trailed after him. He wore an open waistcoat with no shirt beneath, the scar slashing across the column of his throat clearly visible in the bright sunlight. He should be dead with a wound like that.

Nat turned away from it. It wasn't polite to stare. And he probably had to deal with staring and questions about it far too often. It was none of Nat's business.

Their injured arm hurt.

Nat pushed the thoughts that pain triggered away. What was the point of remembering that? This was the reality. They were here. The only option was to make the best of it and move forward.

"You must have a good surgeon aboard," Nat mused, needing to say something, to break the silence— relative silence of the ship in motion.

"What makes you say that?" Aleksei asked from his perch atop the tied-in barrels.

Nat shook a shirt at him. "These are torn to shreds and yet none of you appear to have died yet."

"Most of those are from day to day wear and tear. Coded pirates rarely get into fights."

Coded?

"Oh right?" Nat asked easily, returning to stitching even as their attention fixed entirely on Aleksei.

"Yes," Aleksei responded. "The Code requests we don't fight with one another and, as a general rule, most pirates prefer to avoid the navy."

"Makes sense," Nat agreed. A self-satisfied smile tried to twitch as the corners of their mouth but they pushed it away. Most high society members knew better than to speak so openly with a dandy. It had been a long time since someone was straightforward with Nat. It would be all too easy to let this one brief moment of ease go to their head. They needed to keep a check on their ego, couldn't risk getting cocky. Not here. Not now. Getting cocky risked letting these pirates know their family name. Once they knew, they would send the ransom letter. And then Nat really would be sunk.

"Nobody wants to incur the wrath of the Pirate Queen."

"Of course not."

"Because if you anger the Pirate Queen, you start losing out on the deals in the Pirate Ports."

It wasn't like they didn't enjoy talking entirely in fun, under-layers, and innuendo, but there was definitely a joy in subtly encouraging someone so earnest as Aleksei to spill his knowledge. "And that sucks."

"As Quartermaster, I refuse to pay premium for goods just because my Captain couldn't keep her sword in her pants!"

Nat couldn't help the little snort of laughter that escaped them at that.

Aleksei's head jerked up from his endless knot tying. His eyebrows drew together. "How did you do that?"

Nat's mouth twitched to smile again. "Do what?"

"How did you just get me to give you all that information?"

"Oh, Peaches, you were so desperate to do it."

"How do I manage that?"

Nat laughed.

The little angry part of them, the piece that they tried to ignore and suppress, revelled in the easy banter they shared with Aleksei, the comfortable silence they'd found with Jay. The way they so easily completed their assigned task. All while the bear-man chased Felitabby up and down the deck.

None of the crew of *The Valiant* had been welcoming to Nat when they had joined the crew. Rodgerson and Felitabby particularly, had taken it upon themselves to make Nat's life aboard into a living hell. They set Nat up to fail over and over, getting Nat reprimanded and put on punishment duties. Nat's hands still ached from all that deck swabbing — even in the rain they had had to go out with the mop.

On this pirate ship, they settled more comfortably against the edge of the ship and picked up another shirt to mend. "If you think I'm about to start volunteering my secrets, you've got another thing coming." They smirked up at Aleksei. "But you're welcome to watch an information gathering master at work."

"I can never let you meet Tao," Aleksei muttered.

Nat pressed their tongue to their teeth, keeping that one in reserve for now. Best to wait until Aleksei dropped his guard.

$\mathcal{B}$arely a week of being aboard the pirate ship and it stopped off in a port. Of course, Nat only knew because a few of the pirates had come up to talk to Jay about it in passing. Which meant when Jay gave them an apologetic smile and led them back to their cell in the middle of the day just as land appeared on the horizon, Nat could figure out their little group was about to lose a member.

They had expected it to be Viscount Archin, his parents had more than enough money to pay any ransom requested and it wasn't like the pirates didn't know exactly who he was or where his parents lived.

But no. Archin remained aboard, back in his cell next to Nat.

The one who disappeared from the group was poor, injured Mr Awthorn.

Nat sat quietly in their cell, pressed up against the farthest wall from the other prisoners.

Banter-flirting with Aleksei was fun and, while their fingers hurt from stitching, Nat quite enjoyed having a job to do. Jay was nice enough, quiet and reserved but not so hostile now that xe knew Nat wasn't interested in turning xem into something xe didn't want to be. But Nat was still a prisoner and it wouldn't do to forget such things.

The Captain wanted their family name. She wanted what Nat was worth in money. And the knowledge, bearing the secret that their father wasn't about to pay anyone a ransom for Nat. Let alone pay anything to pirates...

Nat curled their legs up to their chest and wrapped their arms around them. They hid their face in their knees as Felitabby and Archin discussed potential next moves, gossiped about the Awthorn family, and debated how much Jym had gone for.

The ship stilled from motion. Docked.

Nat wanted to go home.

They had wanted to go home since stepping that first foot onto *The Valliant's* boarding plank, wood wobbling under their weight, filling Nat's head with thoughts of crashing into the murky water below. With thoughts of pirates at their back, forcing them to walk the plank and into oblivion. Prophetic it seemed.

Rear-Admiral Eads had been in his office, his cabin, whatever one was meant to call it. He sat behind his desk the exact same way Nat's father did: imposing, larger than life, watching Nat with a dispassionate eye.

Nat had handed the letter over to him. Delivered their own execution order.

He'd opened it, read it, and looked at Nat with something akin to disappointment, to disgust coating his features. Nat was not their father. Nat was frivolously dressed in the swirls and flowers of the season. Nat was weak. Nat was not suitable for the navy.

And that had set up every subsequent interaction aboard *The Valiant.*

It was impossible to tell how much time had passed, though the ship had returned to the particular sway of travel, before footsteps sounded in the cells corridor. Nat swiped a hand over their face, attempting to tidy themself up in any way, shape, or form as keys clanked in the other two occupied cells.

Archin and Felitabby retreated from the room with their respective guards. Nat almost questioned whether they were to be allowed exit from their cells at all. Maybe the Captain had decided their sewing prowess wasn't enough for her liking.

But their door lock clunked.

Nat surged to their feet in a movement that would have been smooth if not for the sea swell that decided to fling the ship to one side at that very moment.

Off balance in more way than one, they crashed straight into Aleksei. His arms wrapped around them, breath ghosting over their face.

Nat's heart leapt into their throat.

Aleksei's tongue darted out to wet his lips. Then those lips pressed softly against Nat's own.

He pulled back. Eyes dark.

"That all you got, Sunflower?" Nat teased.

A flash of teeth told Nat they hadn't been prepared for the response. Quicker than they could register, their back hit the wooden wall. Aleksei's face was close, mere millimetres away from Nat's. His tongue emerged again, drawing his bottom lip into his mouth. Another flash of teeth.

Nat's breath escaped them in an audible sigh, chin tilting up, exposing their neck.

Aleksei's hot breath fanned over the newly revealed skin. His hand crept up, sliding around Nat's cravat, into their hair — longer than they usually kept it thanks to their time at sea. He tilted their head and Nat acquiesced without thought. For once, all thought seemed to have fled their mind.

Lightning sparked down their spine and buzzed in their stomach as Aleksei pressed his lips against Nat's once again. Blunt fingernails scraped over Nat's scalp. The tiniest squeak of a moan escaped Nat as tingling spread over their extremities.

Of their own accord, Nat's hands grabbed hold of Aleksei's waist. The fabric of his shirt caught under their fingers.

Aleksei's teeth nipped at Nat's lower lip.

"Do not silence yourself," he whispered, tongue darting along the shell of Nat's ear.

A tiny "ah" escaped Nat as his tongue and mouth moved down to lick and nibble at their neck.

"Give in to it," he breathed against their neck, hot breath on damp skin.

A deeper moan escaped them. Aleksei's other hand skimmed down their side. It slid until his fingers gripped tightly to Nat's hip, tugging them together, pressing his leg between Nat's.

Nat's head fell back as they gasped for air.

It had been months, *months*, since anyone had touched Nat like this. Their hands travelled up Aleksei's back, gripping his shoulders, his soft tousled hair.

Aleksei bit harder at Nat's neck.

Nat's hands fisted where they were in his hair.

Aleksei moaned; sound vibrating against Nat's throat.

He stopped still, freezing in place. Nat hesitated, gripping fingers loosening. Aleksei cocked his head to one side. When the bellow came again, Nat heard it.

Aleksei huffed out a growl, muttering in Kovian under his breath.

Nat's breath came in ragged pants. Their stomach had turned to liquid and their legs were still jelly.

It had never felt like that when they had fooled around with other ball attendees. Back then, it had been quick fumbles and whispered instructions, all hastily made before emerging from their seclusion with everything put back in its proper place. Now, even though their outer appearance had barely been disturbed, Nat felt more unputtogether than ever.

Aleksei held up a finger. "Stay there," he ordered before stalking off.

Nat's head thumped back against the wooden wall ads they slid down to sit with their knees tucked up against their chest once again.

What were they doing? What were they thinking? How could they be sharing this with a pirate who wanted to ransom them back to their family? A pirate from whom they were keeping more than one big secret? A pirate that, for all Nat knew, might well have been the one who held the jacket his captain had ripped off Nat's shoulders as she set Commander Rodgerson of Her Majesty's Royal Navy to...

Taking a few steadying breaths, Nat clambered to their feet. They knew how this worked. This was hardly their first secret tryst. And they fully intended to save themself the trouble of being caught this time.

They pulled their appearance back together, brushing hands over their hair to encourage it back to where it was supposed to be. Tidying their borrowed and ugly shirt. Rearranging their waistcoat and cravat until they were as sensibly attired as they could be in the situation at hand.

That done, they walked out onto deck and set about stitching shirts.

4
Was This What Freedom Would Feel Like?

Even inexperienced Nat could feel the ship slow as crew members joined together, pulling heavily on a line that had the sail retreating up to its crossbar. Nat frowned from their now-regular stitching position. The wind was buffeting their hair into their face in the direction the ship had been heading. As far as Nat understood it, that was the intended direction of the ship, so why take in the sail?

The Captain stalked across the desk, arms gesturing wildly but too far from Nat for them to hear, her words swept up in the wind as surely as Nat's hair.

Next thing Nat knew, someone dropped down as if from nowhere to directly in front of them, their bare feet barely seemed to touch the deck, almost as if they were floating in front of Nat. "How do you feel about heights?"

"Fine."

"Let's go then." The pirate wrapped a rope around Nat's torso in a practised way, long fingers deft and quick.

"Go where?"

The pirate pointed up to the top of the rigging where the sail was tied in place.

"Whoa, you said heights not climbing."

"Captain's orders," the pirate retorted, as if that were something that just made sense.

"What exactly were those?" Nat hedged.

"Sewing prisoner fixes the sail."

"Is the 'or else' implied?"

"No need to imply. There isn't another option. We do as the Captain orders."

And 'We' apparently now included Nat. Go figure. They gulped but tucked some needles into their shirt cuffs, some thread into their pockets, and followed the pirate to the rough rope rigging.

The pirate that had accosted them scrambled up with no more difficulty than if they were walking on the ground. Nat hauled themself up one stage of the net-like rope ladder. The further they travelled the more their shoulders ached from the pain of keeping themself close, keeping themself upright as they clambered up to the top of the sail. Wind buffeted them from all sides, shaking the rigging under their grip, trying to carry Nat out into the sea.

One foot slipped, sending Nat plummeting toward deck.

The rope around their chest pulled tight around them, shoving the breath out of their lungs.

The rigger appeared in their line of sight, hanging off the rigging in an entirely too comfortable manner. "And that's why we have safety lines."

Nat offered a breathless smile.

"Try again."

Nat swung back toward the rigging, hand reaching and failing to grab the netted rope. Their face burned with embarrassment and shame. It seemed so simple when the rigger did it. They moved with such ease. And Nat couldn't even catch hold!

Finally they managed to grab it well enough to pull themself upright. They took a deep breath, pressing their forehead into one cross hatch of ropes before moving, beginning the climb once again.

The fabric of the sail was pulling away from the rope tying it in place. Nat settled astride the crossbar, locking their ankles together under the bar, just like they had when they had climbed the trees on their family estate, hidden atop branches out of the grip of maids, valets, and valet-maids. The image of bright blue, sparkling eyes and the sound of a child's excitable laughter filled Nat's memory as they leaned down to stitch the proffered piece of canvas into place. Patching the sail.

The wind tried to carry them off as they worked. Tugging bright red swirls of hair in front of their eyes badly enough that they stabbed into their own fingers as often as they managed the sail. A needle disappeared from their grip, either landing somewhere on deck or carried away by the wind. Nat pulled another from their shirt cuff.

Once finished, having done two separate rows of stitching, Nat tugged at the patch with all their might. No point having climbed all the way up here only to have missed an important piece of the puzzle.

They pushed up, peering down at the deck below them. "That is a long way down..."

"Look out instead," the rigger suggested.

Nat tugged their hair out of their face, lifting their head to look out across the sea.

Sunlight sparkled across the peaks of the water as it shifted in an endless movement like the world itself breathed. It went on forever.

For the first time in their life, nothing stood over them.

Was this what freedom would feel like? Could Nat take this feeling with them even as they climbed back down the rigging and settled back into their position, the tiny box that life had seen fit to stuff Nat into?

They took a deep breath of the fresh sea air. "How do you ever come down from here?"

"One foot after the other."

Nat turned to the rigger. "No." They gestured at the view. "From that?"

"I wasn't always called Jay," Jay said, resettling on the barrel nearest Nat with a long piece of rope that had come unwound.

"Oh?" Nat asked, glancing between their current guard-companion and their sewing.

"The Captain and Aleksei rescued me from a naval vessel."

Jay on a naval ship? That was an image that didn't make much sense. The way Jay comported xemself was the antithesis of the naval officers Nat had met. Xe was gentle handed and soft spoken for all the harshness of xyr lingering accent. Jay wouldn't fit on a naval ship. Xe must have been in some real trouble to choose such a life.

"If you're trying to make comparisons between rescue and imprisonment, it seems a little shallow," Nat teased.

"Oh..." Jay's shoulders tensed. Xyr face twisted in a way Nat couldn't quite decipher without more focused attention and pricking themself with a needle killed that possibility. "No I didn't mean it like that. I just..."

Just what? Wanted Nat to reveal their full family name? Was bored? Wanted to build connection? Or could it be that Jay was trying to invite Nat to the possibility of remaining on the ship forever, of petitioning the Captain to let them stay? Never returning back to their home?

"What happened?" Nat asked.

"I had no prospects, got a job as a cook's hand on a ship– turned out to be a navy ship." Jay grimaced.

"Nobody said naval boys had any manners."

"But you're not... like them."

"I don't think you could have paid me a greater compliment than that."

Jay laughed and nudged Nat's shoulder with xyr knee. "I'm bein' honest."

"So am I."

"Sail ho!" the rigger called from somewhere amongst their spider-web of ropes, cutting off Nat and Jay's conversation.

Nat's head snapped up. Across the deck, Felitabby did the same, his eyes boring into them. The mop in his hands clattered to the floor, the sound cracking like thunder across the deck, as he surged toward the edge of the ship.

The pirates around them leapt into motion. Next thing Nat knew they were stuffed back into the cells below deck, Felitabby raging against the bars as the sounds of fighting rose above them. Nat's heart thundered in their ears. Too much like the sound of rain battering the deck. The same sound that had accompanied –no. No no no.

Nat pressed their hands against their temples, as if they could squash the memories out of their heard.

"What are you doing?" Felitabby snarled. "That ship had an Enderand flag; we need to let them know we're here."

The prospect of being rescued only to find themself on another naval ship somehow didn't fill Nat with the same hope it did Felitabby. The haunting command to 'man your fucking post' rang in Nat's ears.

Was this what it would feel like to drown? This breathlessness? The stabbing sort of pain in their lungs? Drowning on dry air like a sea creature taken out of its underwater habitat. Nat's scales had been the jewels of high society, their shoal the dandies they called their friends. And now, far across the known sea from all of that, Nat was alone and Nat was drowning.

5
You Think I Want To Be Here?

The sounds of fighting had faded.
The relative silence of a ship on the sea washing into the cells once again. At some point, both Nat and Felitabby had taken up mirrored positions, sitting with their back to their own walls, knees tucked up. If it weren't for their heads being hidden in their hands, they would have been looking right at one another.

The jingling of keys drew Nat's head up. "You're the one who can stitch, right?"

Nat nodded.

"Great." The pirate unlocked the door and tugged Nat gently to their feet. "We need you in the surgery."

"Surgery?" Nat yelped. "I'm not a doctor."

"A stitch is a stitch." The same words they'd spoken to the Captain.

"I really don't think that it is in this case." But the pirate didn't listen, just dragged Nat into the surgery. Yet another bland wooden space like every other room below deck Nat had ever seen.

Beds had been laid out in a single neat line. There weren't enough for all the injured pirates loitering in the room.

"I brought you the..."

"Dandy," Nat supplied to fill the pause.

The surgeon, an aging woman with more silver in her hair than the black it had once been, spoke in a language Nat didn't recognise. She handed them a tray and gestured at the more mildly injured set of pirates.

Nat took the tray over to a corner with a chair and small table. They arranged the contents of the tray into something like a logical order. That same kind of alcohol to wipe clean wounds, a needle and thread, and clean, if stained, bandages.

The first pirate sat in front of them, apparently unbothered that Nat was one of the prisoners. Or at least willing to risk it to cease bleeding.

Nat's hands shook as they cleaned the wound across the pirate's ribs.

"You going to make me mend that shirt too?" they teased, clinging to their dandy persona in the desperate attempt to make this whole situation less... what it was.

The pirate shot Nat a flash of a smile.

They threaded the curved needle. They hadn't even seen a curved needle before! Taking a deep, alcohol scented breath, they pressed the skin together. It's just like stitching fabric. Stitching wet, meaty fabric.

They swallowed thickly and began.

It was nothing like stitching fabric.

But when the first pirates was done and bandaged up and accepted Nat's assessment that the shirt was for the rubbish pile not the mending pile with another flash of a smile, the next pirate took up the vacated spot and offered Nat another injury to clean, stitch and bandage.

By the time the vast majority of the pirates had cleared out of the surgery, leaving only the few who needed further care from a trained and professional doctor, Nat was trembling with exhaustion.

The ship's surgeon clapped a hand on their shoulder, speaking once again in that language Nat couldn't figure out. They shook their head, helplessly.

"Food, drink, sleep," she clarified.

Nat stumbled up onto the deck and right into the Captain railing on Archin. "I'm saying it looks suspicious that we're setting up to exchange you for your ransom when we're besieged by the navy." Her hand landed on the weapon on her belt. "Tell me why it's worth my while to not kill you now."

"My parents have agreed to pay," Archin offered. It sounded like a question more than a statement.

The Captain's sword sparkled in the lantern light shining on deck.

"Seems pointless to have come this far only to give up now," Nat muttered.

The Captain spun on them, sword snicking all the way back into its scabbard as she folded her arms. "I don't appreciate being interrupted."

Nat lifted their bloodied hands, stumbling without the security of the wall they had previously been resting against. "I got lost."

"Kajal, take that one back down to the cells." The words were spoken in the same tone she seemed to say everything else.

The rigger launched themself down to stand beside Nat, linking their arms together. They hadn't even turned away from the deck before the Captain continued her interrogation of Archin.

Would his parents have risked sending the navy before the trade had been made? Or was this unrelated?

$\mathcal{N}$at pressed their forehead against a cross-hatch of bars, just as they had against the rigging. How had that been three whole days ago? They and Felitabby had been locked back into their cells as land approached the horizon.

Viscount Archin's parents had obviously paid his increased and undoubtedly handsome ransom. Nat was almost surprised. It had taken long enough that they were starting to believe his parents had taken the same stance Nat's own would should they ever receive a ransom note. Not that they would. Not if Nat had any say in the matter.

Knowing you would be abandoned was a different situation than experiencing it.

Nat sighed.

Felitabby rattled the door of his cell. It had taken the bear-sized man and an incredibly muscular woman who had made Nat's brain melt just a little to wrestle him into the cell in the first place.

He shouted and screamed.

"Would you just shut up!" Nat snapped, jerking their head toward him, eyes narrowed to glare.

"Me?" Felitabby snapped back.

"You think this is any easier for me than it is for you? You think I want to be here anymore than you do?"

"Why not just tell them your name and be done with it?"

"Why don't you!"

Felitabby's mouth snapped shut with an audible clack. "We've been in rough financial shape."

Nat had known that, but they decided not to share. Why else would their eldest son have enlisted in the navy? "So it's not just your pride?"

The silence hung heavy. Ah, a little of both perhaps. Felitabby knew his family likely couldn't afford to pay a ransom and, even if they could scrounge up the funds, he didn't want them to have to. He didn't want to be the thing that put them deeper into debt. And he didn't want to need rescuing.

"You've settled in all nice," he sneered.

"I know how to manipulate people, it's what we do."

"We?"

"Dandies."

Felitabby snorted. "Dandies faint and wear ridiculous clothes and fail to manage even the most basic physical activity."

"Dandies set fashion trends and trade in information."

"They corrupt young gentlemen into improper activities."

"Improper activities? F—" Nat cut themself off before Felitabby's surname came out. "Thomin, are you talking about—"

"Intimacies!"

Nat couldn't hold in their laugh. "Those kinds of activities are done by almost every married couple in the world, regardless of gender or dandy status."

"Pre-marital intimacies."

"I thought young men were encouraged to engage in such activities?"

"Well... Yes. But..."

"It's okay if you don't want to, you know that, right? If you never want to. That's perfectly normal."

"What would you know?"

Nat shrugged. "Like I said, I trade in information. And, for the record, since we're already having this incredibly uncomfortable conversation, I have no such interest in you."

Felitabby snorted again.

"You think highly of yourself."

"Why shouldn't I? I am from a well-regarded family, have proven my naval prowess, and would be able to provide. I am a catch."

"A catch for someone looking to marry, perhaps. A catch for someone who didn't serve on the same ship as you, perhaps." A catch for someone who hadn't been bullied almost to breaking point by him and his friend, perhaps.

"It's not like you'd be able to avoid marriage."

"I should hope to only enter into such an agreement with someone I actually liked, Thomin. I'm not necessarily hoping for love or anything, I'm no fool. But at least someone tolerable."

"And I'm not?"

"Not to me."

"I can't believe the Archins paid up..."

Nat hummed. The Archin family was flush. It wasn't like they didn't have the funds, that was why Archin's extended stay had been such a surprise. Surely they would have paid as early as Mr Awthorn's family. Unless Awthorn wasn't ransomed at all and was, instead, abandoned in some hospital somewhere.

It didn't bear thinking about.

6
You Have No Place In This World

The evening after losing Archin, Nat had been abandoned on the deck, tucked in the shadows behind the barrels that Aleksei perched upon when he was set to guarding them. They'd either garnered enough trust that their guard had felt safe to leave them alone or they had just been forgotten, either way the ship was dark but for the swinging lanterns attached to the masts to illuminate the ship enough to walk around on.

Their eyes burned with fatigue, fingers clumsy and aching from overuse.

Their guard for that day hadn't been talkative. No chatting, no banter, no nothing. Nat couldn't face the thought of returning to those cells by their own volition. They couldn't bear the thought of Felitabby finally attempting to include them in his escape plans, nor the idea that he wouldn't bother to include them at all.

What did Felitabby expect to do on this ship full of pirates? Especially considering the fact that said pirates had already successfully abducted him once, from a naval ship at that.

No. Nat didn't want to be part of his plans. But the idea of being left behind... Not that Nat had ever been the type someone fought for. Fought against, maybe. But not for.

That was fine. Nat could figure it out on their own. They'd been doing that long enough now. This was hardly different. Except for the pirate part... the middle of the sea part... Still. All they needed to do for now was survive. Survive, prove themself useful enough to keep around, and not let on who their family was.

A shadow loomed over them and Nat looked up to find the bear of a man.

He grunted.

Nat offered a sheepish smile. "Good evening."

He grunted again.

For the briefest instant, Nat's attention caught on the scar across his neck. They refocused on his face. "Do you sign?" they asked, clumsily putting together what little sign language they knew into the words 'you' and 'sign'. How did one go about asking questions again? There was a specific sign for that, wasn't there?

He blinked and nodded slowly.

"I'm not very good," Nat offered. Speaking and signing. "But I know some —no, wait, that was believe." Nat looked at their hands as they searched their brain for the sign for 'know'.

Movement pulled their attention up to the bear man. He had perched on the edge of the barrel Aleksei also sat on. "I can hear," he signed with fluency. "You don't have to sign."

"I guessed. I just remember better with my hands."

He smiled. It suited him, softened his face in a way that made him seem all the more human and less bear-like. "You should be asleep."

Nat shook their head. They couldn't do it. They couldn't go back to that cell and lie on the floor across from Felitabby and attempt to sleep. Their endless, ever-racing brain wouldn't allow it, wouldn't slow down enough for Nat to turn it off. Nights like this in their life before the sea, Nat would have never returned from the social event that had called them out for the evening. They would have stayed out until the brushes of dawn painted the horizon, peered between buildings in Dinium's centre. They would have hailed an early morning cab and headed back home in time to change for family breakfast and suffered through holding in yawns for the entire next day.

Now, to the pirate, they gestured at the pile of shirts. "I have too much to do."

The bear-man folded his arms over his barrel of a chest.

"Can I ask you a question?"

He looked away, hand flashing to cover his scar.

"Why don't you wear a shirt?"

He paused. Obviously not the question he was expecting. The hand covering his scar shifted to rub at the base of his neck. "It chafes."

"Because of the movement?"

He nodded.

Nat finished tying off the stitches on the shirt they had just mended. "May I try something?"

Hesitantly the bear-man nodded.

Nat slipped the waistcoat off his shoulders with gentle fingers. His skin was warm even in the cool night air. They set the waistcoat atop the pile of mended shirts and helped him into a suitable shirt. They buttoned it all the way to the top, using cautious and careful hands near his scar. Whatever happened to cause it, Nat didn't want to bring him discomfort.

They whipped off their own cravat, tying it in an elegant but simple knot around the collar of the newly mended shirt, settling the fabric in place before replacing the waistcoat — taking the time to pick out a button to replace the one missing from the very middle of it.

He touched a hand to his newly covered neck. The scar still peeked out the top, just a little, far less jarring and attention grabbing than it had been before.

"Is that... okay?" Nat asked, stepping away. "I'm not saying you have to cover it up or anything, I just thought you might want—"

The bear-man took Nat's hands in his, cutting off their rambling. Tears gathered in his eyes. "Thank you."

It was as if the words lifted a physical weight from Nat's shoulders. Their smile was broken by a yawn.

"Bed."

"Do you have a name?"

"I did... before..." He touched the cravat.

Nat didn't ask whether it was that he couldn't spell it or that he wanted to distance himself from it. If he wanted to talk about it with them, he would do it on his own. "I mean what do people call you?"

"Hey, you," the signs were sharp.

Nat winced. "What do you want to be called?"

He shrugged.

"Well," Nat yawned again. "Let me know if that changes. I'd like to stop mentally calling you 'the bear-man' if at all possible."

*N*at stood, stretching out their aching back against the edge of the ship's railing, when something shining caught their eye. Was that purple? What kind of sea creature had purple scales?

Nat jerked when they spotted the arm. They spun to find Jay. But xe had gone off to do something urgent, trusting Nat to stay where they were in the meantime. Where else could Nat go in the middle of the ocean?

They scrabbled for the nearest crew member, for once unable to find the words to communicate. They dragged her to the edge of the ship and pointed out into the water.

"Overb—" she began, cutting herself off as realisation broke out over her face. It twisted into horror. "Sirens!"

Sirens? Nat's eyes blew wide as their attention shifted back to the water and the shining purple scales. They gripped the railing with white knuckled fists, clinging desperately to the semblance of safety that was remaining on the ship, even as their eyes played over the water. Searching.

Her head appeared above the water, eyes as black as pitch. No pupil, no iris, no nothing. Just blackness. She smiled, mouth closed, full lips stretching pleasantly. One hand appeared from the water, held out to Nat. Inviting.

Somebody grabbed Nat by the back of their shirt, yanking them away from the edge of the ship.

"I'm hardly about to let you get eaten by sirens," the Captain snapped, shoving Nat up against the main mast, and wrapping rope around their waist to secure them there.

From the white crested waves the song began. A deeply reverent sound unlike anything Nat had ever heard. Full of longing and with a distinctly mournful quality. A cry for connection and love and the basest of understandings.

Nat pressed their back against the mast behind them, fingers digging into the wood, trying to ground themself in something physical, something other than that haunting melody. That sound that encompassed everything Nat had so long felt.

"You have no place in this world," it seemed to say. "Come, find your place among the waves."

Nat closed their eyes, lest their composure break and they begin to cry.

The Slosh Of A Wave Upon A Broken Piece Of Ship

Nat had ascertained at a young age that they were too much. Too much for their parents, who scrambled to keep up with the way they spoke, the way they acted, even more so after their mother had died. Too much for their tutors and the other household staff set to taking care of Nat. The amount of times Nat had become tired of lessons and disappeared from them to explore the grounds, returning with pine cones and bugs or even just scrapes on their hands and knees. Even on their best behaviour, in their concentrated form, unfiltered and unguarded, Nat was a summer storm, sweeping in and making a mess. Impossible to avoid and impossible to deal with. It was part of why they had chosen a storm-like pattern for their tattoo.

They had learnt their best choice was to smush that too-muchness down into its own little box. Become compliant and quiet.

Coming out to society, Nat had hoped things might change. That someone not subjected to them at all hours of the day or in such a contractual way might find their too-muchness endearing. But it hadn't worked. Nat had continued their compliant act to the best of their ability. Desperate to prevent their too-muchness from spilling over and making messes Nat didn't know how to get out of.

It worked. Most of the time. Sometimes impulse struck with such ferocity that Nat had no hope of controlling it. Couldn't recognise it before it was too late. Thus the almost-scandal that had sent them to sea. Thus the undoing of the ropes tying them to the main mast in the middle of siren territory.

The siren song had lasted most of the day. Unfavourable winds kept the ship from moving on. As the sun had set and the pirates, all their ears plugged with wax, had set about heading for their respective beds, it had dwindled.

Nat and Felitabby were left on deck with only the night guard for company. Not much by way of company, actually, with her plugged ears. Still, better than Felitabby whose eyes had turned glassy almost immediately as the siren song began. His desperation had only increased as the music weighed on them all.

The ropes had slackened over the course of the day. Nat may have been on a navy ship less than a year, but even they knew these knots weren't going to hold anything, let alone a persistent dandy. Nat had experienced more effective knots in high society!

When the night guard strolled away, lantern swinging, Nat slipped out of the ropes.

Technically they didn't need to be quiet with the night guard's plugged ears, but they weren't about to take any chances.

They tucked themself into a corner where the railing hadn't been boarded up. The area usually covered by barrels to collect rainwater. It was a tight squeeze but nothing too uncomfortable. Plus, it was the only area of the deck secreted from easy view with ease of sight of the sea. If it had been Nat's ship, none of these railings would have been boarded, especially not in such an ugly manner. What was wrong with railings with space between them?

"Hello?" Nat called over the quiet, still sea.

Nothing responded. Maybe they had managed to get out of siren territory after all. The stars glittered over the water, everything unnaturally still in the cool air.

Nat sighed. Just their luck. One glimpse of sirens and gone all too soon. They shifted off their knees to lean their back against the wall of the upper bow. It was probably for the best. Sirens were treacherous, dangerous, deadly. But, then again, so were pirates.

"I never even got to see a tail."

"I'm sure we can fix that if you come down here," a voice called. It echoed with remnants of waves, more layers than a human voice could ever boast.

Nat started.

Once again, a pair of dark eyes examined Nat from just above the water.

"I'm afraid I can't come down there right now," Nat said, slipping ever-so-easily into their dandy tone and words. "Why don't you come up here instead?"

The siren laughed, sharp teeth flashing over the top of the water.

A shiver trickled down Nat's spine. They really needed to stop being so impulsive. "I hear sirens have the best voices on the planet," Nat complimented. "But nobody ever warned me of your eyes."

"You could see them better if you came closer."

"Are you truly that hungry for a scrawny little thing like me?"

"All those who pass through our waters are fair prey."

Trespassing. Nat shook off the memory of sheeting rain, of the pain that night had brought. They were here now and it wouldn't do to get distracted doing something as risky as talking with a siren. "I take it you never allow treaties then?"

"Treaties?"

"Accords, safety in return for something else."

"What could we want that a human would be able to provide?"

Nat thought on that. What could a human provide to sirens that they would want more than food? That was if the stories were to be believed and the sirens wanted humans as food and not for some other purpose. "Stories?" Nat suggested. "Songs?"

"We have our own."

"Well, obviously. Everybody has their own songs and stories. But sometimes it's nice to hear stories and songs from somewhere else."

The siren blinked slowly. "Perhaps... if you were captain of this vessel you could barter for such a thing."

"And you know me not to be?"

"We know many things, walking cash."

"Nat."

The siren's head tilted.

"My name. It's Nat, not walking cash."

"I am the slosh of a wave upon a broken piece of ship."

"Long title. Do you go by anything shorter, The Slosh Of A Wave Upon A Broken Piece Of Ship?"

This time the smile came out sharp and fangy. "Wave."

Nat smiled even as the hairs on the back of their neck stood on end. "It's a pleasure to meet you, Wave."

"I believe you truly mean that."

"It's always a pleasure to meet someone from a background different to one's own."

"Even if they have fangs."

"Even if they have dishonourable intentions."

A laugh with more layers than Nat could truly hear, something that set off some instinctive part of them in a way they could barely understand internally, a thrill mixed with the edge of fear that raised the hairs on the back if Nat's neck while simultaneously sending warmth swirling in their stomach.

"Offer me one," Wave said. "And I will convince my shoal to allow your ship its freedom. Just this once."

"One what?"

"One story or song. I wish to try this trade."

Nat licked their lips. They had offered without thinking. Now they had to come up with something to share, something a siren would find appealing enough to agree was worth losing out on a whole ship's worth of presumably tasty pirates. "Okay, I heard this in the Swallow Song back home." Nat settled themself more comfortable, sliding their legs to hang between the railings over the side of the ship. Flirting with the danger of the sirens below. "And I should warn you, I'm not the most practised singer."

Nat counted out the introduction in their head before launching into the song itself. A folksy tune that had resounded in the small pub with the delicate stained glass window. They let their eyes close, picturing the Swallow's Song interior.

A warm fire crackling in the fireplace, lighting the room in gentle orange. The carpet had once been patterned but was faded from use. They would probably avoid replacing it until it had worn through to the floor beneath. Each of the chairs was mismatched, picked for their comfort more than their design. Nat's favourite had been an old wood and leather thing with brass studs and less padding than it probably should have had.

The musicians that had sung the song were a duo, an instrument in each of their hands. Their clothes hadn't matched anything Nat had ever seen before, clearly cultural in some way, but Nat hadn't been able to place it at the time. The music carried well over the room, even with the quiet murmur of conversation. In fact it seemed to have been composed with the intention of playing over conversation.

On the table in front of Nat could have sat any number of meals from the Swallow

Song. But always a freshly baked and still warm bread roll. No matter your choice, the bread roll would appear and a small dish of butter to spread over it. It warmed the heart— and the hands on a cold day.

By the time Nat was nearing the end of what they remembered of the song, more than they had expected to for something so fleetingly heard, more heads had popped up from the rippling water.

They began to copy the echo Nat had filled in for themself. Some even going so far as to lend harmonies to the chorus or quiet hums like the instrumentals.

A hand wrapped around Nat's arm. They let out a shriek as it dragged them across the deck and to their feet.

"What do you think you're doing?" the night guard yelled as the sirens hissed in the water, faces distorting into a terrifying visage.

Nat tried to break free from the grip on their arm where it dug into the still-sensitive cuts. "Bartering."

"What?"

Right. Blocked ears. "Bartering."

"Bartering?"

"For safe passage."

When the night guard frowned and opened her mouth to ask what Nat had said again Nat held up a hand. "If you want to have a conversation, Peaches, you might consider unplugging your ears." They made the motion of taking something away from their own ears.

Hesitantly she pulled one plug from her ear.

"Much better," Nat sighed, though they were still trapped in her strong grip. It pressed against their injured arm. Warmth bloomed there. Had she re-opened the cuts? "I was bartering for our safe passage."

"What? How?" She narrowed her eyes. "Why?"

"What? Bartering by having a conversation and offering trade. How? By singing a song: the agreed upon trade. Why? Because, shockingly enough, I don't want to be eaten by sirens any time soon."

"But you're not crew."

"No."

"Then why?"

Nat tried not to roll their eyes. "I already told you, Peaches. I do not wish to be eaten by sirens any time soon."

"Then why risk a conversation with them at all?"

Ah, the eternal question. Why did Nat do half the things they did? The desperate dandified desire to learn more about the thing that made them afraid. The same thing that had made them flirt with Aleksei that first day in the cell. The same thing that had handed their cravat over to Bear. Poorly quashed impulse.

They glanced at Felitabby. He was still visibly addled but had, at least, exhausted himself into an awkward sleep. Why had he been so affected and Nat had been so reluctant? Maybe it was to do that with impulse. Maybe not. Maybe it was because Nat knew how to indulge in something. Feeling or impulse or whatever they so chose and Felitabby was wound tighter than a spring toy.

The shrugged. "It was worth an attempt."

"We would have managed to sail out eventually."

Nat shrugged. Maybe. But maybe sirens really could control the weather in their territories like it said in the books Nat had read about them. Maybe they couldn't. And maybe Nat just extricated themself from their binding because being eaten by sirens couldn't be worse than what the pirates had in mind when they found out Nat's father wouldn't pay their ransom.

8
Who Says I Fight Fair?

The sun beat down on the deck, heat pressing against Nat, light shining over the wood. It had been like this since leaving Siren waters; low wind and baking heat. Acquiescing to the pressure of it, Nat folded up the too-long sleeves of their borrowed shirt, past their elbows, giving up that smidge of propriety to the unrelenting heat. Propriety was pretty much all gone since they had gifted bear-man their cravat.

Aleksei fanned himself with a hand, blowing out a huge breath. "It's too hot."

"Hot enough for rolled up sleeves," Nat muttered, pulling at the thread with their teeth. They would never have got away with that in high society; one did not put things other than food and food utensils in their mouths. It was something Nat's little sister had used to do, endlessly corrected by her tutors and governesses that she needed to reach for the scissors only for them to tell her off immediately after for reaching too far for the scissors.

Nat pressed their fingers tighter to the fabric, grounding themself in the moment. Don't think about her. Don't picture that perfect beaming smile. Don't imagine the softness of her hair every time she came to get it fixed. Don't remember the tiny rebellions or the good behaviours: walking the grounds, practicing piano, playing party in the ballroom having both abandoned their shoes by the door. Nat hadn't seen their sister since being sent to sea and they had to assume they would never see her again. The needle snapped.

"I didn't think you high society types did that," Aleksei said.

"Rolled up our sleeves?" Nat asked, shaking out their battered fingers.

"No, that." He gestured at Nat's forearm.

Nat looked at the tattoo on their arm, exposed in a way it never would have been in high society, as if they were surprised it was there. As if they didn't already know exactly what it looked like nestled just below the crook of the elbow. Only just peeking out from under their badly re-wound bandages.

"Oh, yeah." They looked up at Aleksei. "It happens."

"It happens?"

"Us high society types do get them."

"Any specific purpose behind it?"

Nat looked down at the tattoo again. It had been Liege Mishra that had invited them to get it. Xe had shown Nat xyr own, tucked into the curve of xyr hip bone: ivy vines in the same twisting circle that every person in the group got. Nat's was made up of swirling colour, indistinct lines almost like a storm as seen from above.

Liege Mishra had explained that the point was to show that they worked primarily on the fringes of society. That dandies such as them were unlikely to ever be truly welcomed into the centre, so they had made the edges a pleasant and purposeful space for themselves. Xe had explained that this tradition had been running for longer than anyone could trace, that xe had been invited just like Nat was being now.

Rajni had one too. Hers was a peacock feather. And placed closer to her wrist, easy to hide under even short gloves.

"Nothing that would hold meaning for you," they said to Aleksei.

"But it means something to you?"

"Don't all tattoos hold meaning for the people who get them?"

The relentless heat only continued as the days passed on. Crew members grew restless, water grew scarcer – Aleksei kept walking to the water barrels stored on deck, opening the top, frowning, and resealing them. Nat had tried everything, stretching out so their body touched itself as little as possible, scrunching up in a desperate attempt to remain in what little comfort there was to be found in the shadows. Their skin had turned as red as their hair and itched with burn.

A rope snapped, the clap of it thundering over the ship. It flung out by Nat's face and, out of some misguided instinct, they grabbed it.

Their legs roared with protest as the rope dragged them to their feet and then from them.

The world distorted. Which way was up? Nat really didn't want to vomit into the sky. Not that they wanted to vomit at all. But into the sky would surely be far worse. They desperately flailed for something to grab. Their hand connected with a forearm. They gripped. Fingers dug into their arm in turn, yanking them to a shoulder-popping stop even as they still didn't release the rope.

"Fuck me!" The person holding Nat whistled. "That was amazing. Why did you do that?"

Nat swallowed down their nausea, trying to meet those sparkling ocean blue eyes around their spinning, circling vision. It wasn't the rigger, someone else lingering on the twisted rope nets. They probably had a job too.

"Seemed like a good idea at the time."

Ocean-eyes laughed, a bright sound more akin to a wind chime than a real laugh and tugged Nat onto the rigging with them. They took the rope from Nat's hands, palms turned as red and burned as the rest of them.

Nat was still trying to make it down the rigging without embarrassing themself, breath hissing between their teeth at the press of new pain against their palms, when they caught the tail of a conversation.

"There's a big storm coming, we need to dock before then," Aleksei said.

"And where do you suggest we do that? Considering we're currently holding cash in person form?" the Captain replied.

"The closest port is Shenai."

"We can't take two of them to Shenai."

"Then we need to get them ransomed back. Fast."

"They won't tell us their family names." A different voice. Jay? No, someone who sounded like Jay. Jay was still where Nat had been mending shirts before they'd been taken away by the runaway rope.

"Then we apply pressure," the Captain snapped. "Aleksei, you can use your particular advantages on the soft one."

"Yes, Captain." No argument. Not even a hesitation.

Nat closed their eyes, taking a deep breath to steel themself. The soft one. That was... a title.

Their fingers ached from stitching. Their hands burned from grabbing the rope. Their shoulders cried out for attention from the ungainly wrenching off their feet. And that wasn't even acknowledging their still-bandaged arm, which Nat was steadfastly ignoring in favour of pretending it didn't exist.

Soft wasn't something they felt.

Their feet touched down on the deck of the ship. Kajal, the rigger, climbing like a spider across all those ropes turned and shot Nat a brief wave.

Gently, Nat stretched out their aching shoulders, only to find themself crowded up against the main mast.

"Hi," Aleksei greeted, breath ghosting over Nat's ear.

Nat pressed their tongue against their teeth, almost biting down on it to keep their initial feelings to themself.

Aleksei was still appealing from a purely lust-ridden standpoint. From the position of wanting what little pleasure could be found on a pirate ship. The briefest respite from the desperate loneliness that clung to Nat.

But, knowing his Captain had set him to the task for a purpose, to try and coax Nat into telling them everything, put a real icy shower on the whole situation. And it brought a few too many questions about consent into the matter at that. Did he really want to do this with Nat? Had he ever? Should it even surprise them that such a supposedly simple question could be mired in such confusion?

But Nat didn't go in for this kind of thing if the others involved weren't actively, intentionally invested in it. Not to soften the aching loneliness. Not to trade in information. Not to cling to what little pleasure could be found in such an awful environment. Not if their partners didn't want to. Not if they were only there for some ulterior motive. Not if someone else had told them to be. Not even with pirates.

"I'd rather you didn't," Nat whispered. "Not like this."

Aleksei stepped back, a crease between his brows.

Nat pushed past him and returned to their station, limbs trembling in a way that had little to do with their recent de-gravitisation and a lot more to do with refusing Aleksei.

For all that they had rules; Nat had never been very good at saying no. Never been good at turning down a prospect. They'd heard every word for it, every title one could give a person like that, positive ones and negative ones. Easy. Slut. Ruiner. Ruined. Fun. Disaster. They always responded the same way: a joke, a laugh, giving the appearance that the words slid off them like water off a duck.

Eventually the words had stopped hurting. They weren't inaccurate, after all. Nat was easy. They liked pleasure. And they found it where it was offered. Where it was wanted.

But, then, it wasn't just sex that Nat was bad at saying no to.

Aleksei approached Nat's working area while their trembling fingers failed to pick up any of the fabric.

Jay looked between him and Nat and promptly lifted a hand to xyr ear and dashed off below deck. Traitor.

"What do you mean by that?" Aleksei demanded.

"I mean, if you think you're going to addle me into telling you things by kissing me silly, you're sorely mistaken."

"I..."

Nat offered him a flat smile. "And, ultimately, the fact that you would so readily reach for that without even bothering to try out-and-out asking first is, frankly, a little ridiculous."

"I did ask."

"On our first meeting." Nat raised an eyebrow. "Considering the position I was in, did you really expect me to give you everything you wanted back then?"

"Would you have told me? If I asked now?"

"Of course not." Nat rolled their eyes.

"Then what would be the point?"

"Honour, Aleksei. A fight is only fair if all parties know they are fighting."

"I'm a pirate, who says I fight fair?"

Nat pressed their tongue to their teeth again, tracing the sharp edge of one canine. They shrugged one shoulder. "I thought the rules might be different between us."

"You have just established that there is no us."

"Are you truly so bitter that your walking cash has taken a stand against being ruined? That can happen to Lieges too, you know. Ruin. Perhaps the trade-off is too pricey now."

"If you're that worried about ruin, wouldn't you want to be returned to your family as soon as possible?"

"Or maybe being on a pirate ship at all is too much ruin for me to ever return," Nat fired back. The needle, still halfway through a stitch bit into their thumb and they hissed as they stuck the bleeding appendage into their mouth. "Face it, Peaches. You don't know anything about me and you can't make accurate judgements from a place of ignorance."

"Peaches again?"

Nat smiled up at him, the most dandified smile they could muster. "It's what I call people I don't like."

9

It's What We Do

Land appeared on the horizon, shimmering in the heat haze. Nat watched it. Pausing their stitches. Longing to be off the sea filled them like a pitcher of water. To stand on flat land, feel the ground beneath their feet, to be anywhere but a ship.

Nat had never wanted to spend any amount of time on ships. They had been content to read about other people's explorations, to experience none of their own. They had been perfectly content in high society; balls and dinners and other events, running the rumour mill at the edges of the dance floor, and flirting the line of impropriety.

A hand landed on their shoulder, cementing them in the current moment in time. On a pirate ship. Trapped at sea. And completely alone. "Time to go below," Jay said.

"As always," Nat sighed. They followed Jay toward the door to the lower decks, shooting one last longing look at the shimmering horizon.

Jay locked the door behind Nat, reaching through the bars to squeeze their fingers in xyr own. Almost an apology. Even as Felitabby wrestled with a pair of bulky pirates trying to force him into his own cell.

The pirates disappeared from the room and Felitabby kicked the door to his cell, making all the bars clatter and sing.

The space felt different with just the two of them, with the way their lives had shifted and changed aboard the ship. The distance of two, simple, empty cells between them stretched as far as the horizon. Impossible to cross. Still, Nat tried.

"They're getting desperate," they whispered, once the ringing died down.

"What?"

"The pirates. They don't want us on board when they arrive in port to wait out the storm."

"What storm?"

"I don't know. I heard them talking about it."

"You think I'm going to take the word of a dandy, Liege—"

"I would rather you keep that name out of your mouth, my Lord," Nat interrupted, voice harsh. They had hardly put all that work into concealing their identity only for Thomin Felitabby to give it away now.

"There's nobody else here."

"I'm sure that's what the Captain thought when she was discussing heading for Shenai."

"We're going to Shenai?"

"That's what I heard."

"Shit."

"What?"

"There's a known Pirate Port in Shenai." He said the words Pirate Port like they were a real title, not just descriptors.

"What do you mean?"

"A Pirate Port, a Port for Pirates. The Unknown World."

"How unknown can it be if there's ports there?"

Felitabby gave Nat one last disparaging look and kicked the bars. "Let me out!"

Nat rolled their eyes and leaned back against the solid wall behind them. This was going to be a long port stay, especially if they had to remain below deck with Felitabby the entire length of a storm that hadn't even struck yet.

The person shaped shadow loomed over Nat even as far away as the doorway to the cells. They peered up from tying and retying the frayed edges of their borrowed shirt sleeve. One too many needles stuck through and it had started to fall to pieces. A shame they couldn't just take one of the countless shirts from the mended pile for themself. Not that any of them held particular appeal, all that same old fashioned style with the too-wide shoulders and cuffs that would flop over Nat's hands. Nat hadn't felt this uncomfortable in their clothing and, by extension, their body since the original onset of puberty. That had been a particularly tough time.

Aleksei lingered in the opening, almost as if he wasn't sure whether he wanted to enter the room or not.

Nat glanced at Felitabby's cell. He let out a wheeze of a snore. Figured he wouldn't be interested in forging an escape plan with Nat when they were most able to escape. They were going to have to stay docked for the entirety of the storm. Now was the perfect, possibly only, time this would be possible. And Thomin was sleeping through it.

Maybe his plan hinged on night time starts. Though how one would tell it was night time in a windowless cell below deck, Nat didn't know. Could be some other naval knowledge they weren't privy to. Or Thomin might just be a fool.

Aleksei surged forward, boots scuffing quietly against the worn wood. "I'm sorry," he whispered, turning the key in the lock eakingly slowly so it wouldn't clang. "You were right. I should never have used that method, I just..." He pulled the cell door open enough for Nat to squeeze out.

"You do as your captain bids. I know. That's how ships work."

"How did you know that's what I was doing?"

"I'm a dandy, Sunflower. It's what we do."

With another quick glance at the sleeping Lord, Aleksei grabbed Nat's hand and tugged them from the room.

The sun was still blindingly bright on deck. Before Nat's vision could adjust the ground under their feet changed. Unsteady, usturdy to sudden stone.

Still Aleksei didn't let them stop. He tugged Nat through bustling streets. Their vision cleared to allow them to take in the various sizes of building with flat and arched rooves and shining gold embellishments. People of every possible configuration bustled around, eating food, talking, carting cargo.

Nat almost tugged Aleksei to a halt. People. Land. Reality.

"Come on," he encouraged, chivvying them into motion once again.

How could they begin to explain how long it had been since Nat stood on land.

Since Nat had seen beyond the crew of a ship — or two ships, they supposed.

Aleksei tugged Nat through a market square and up onto a wooden outcropping, a patio of sorts.

The bustle inside the tavern assaulted Nat on all sides. Though their time on ships had been brief in the grand scheme of their life, it had been so all-consuming and left no lingering familiarity with such establishments. Not that this particular tavern had much by way of similarity to any Nat had visited.

Languages from all corners of the known and unknown world filtered together with the undercurrent drumbeat of feet shifting and tankards being placed on surfaces. Aleksei's hand was warm in Nat's. A comfort. An anchor. And yet somehow still a reminder of the precarious position they were in.

He led them around tables and groups toward his intended destination, booths in the back corner, somewhat hidden from the doorway.

Someone leapt to stand with one foot on the table and one on the seat of a chair. The amber liquid inside their tankard swished out, spilling across the floor in a white foam. Words erupted from their mouth in a catchy tune.

With a rapidity Nat could barely believe, the musicians on the stage picked up the melody to accompany them.

Another voice, across the room, repeated a line.

The first person continued.

Nat stopped still. Captivated.

Aleksei's hand slipped from theirs. The bustle of the tavern filling the space between them.

The tune and lyrics skipped around the room like an intriguing piece of gossip at a dance. And, as so often happened with the gossip, someone offered it to Nat.

For an instant, just the thump of their heart against their rib cage, Nat froze. Uncertain. Were they meant to sing? Would anyone join them? What if they got it wrong?

But that proffered hand and smiling stranger were too inviting for Nat to ignore. They'd never been good at saying no. They took the extended hand and let the pirate drag them up onto the table.

When Nat left off their verse, the chorus rang out as the majority of the tavern took up what Nat had offered. Their smile threatened to break their face as they let the inviting pirate parade them around the room in a semblance of a dance unlike any dance Nat had shared before.

As the song wound to a close, Nat spun in the pirate's arms to grin up at her. "Thanks."

She offered a nod and released Nat from her grip.

They stumbled only slightly, orientating themself in the strange place. Aleksei had tucked himself into the booth he had been heading for originally. Nat made their way over to him.

He pushed a tankard over the table toward them. "I had thought you would just be happy to leave the ship but I should have guessed you'd get caught up."

Nat raised an eyebrow.

"Not a complaint. Just recognising my own foolishness."

"Do tell," Nat invited. They sipped at the tankard, grimacing to find something bitter and biting within.

"You're not the kind to sit on the side-lines and watch; you're the type to throw in. It's obvious and I ignored it."

Nat frowned into the foamy amber liquid in their tankard. Was that true? Dandies were supposed to stand on the side-lines and gather information. That was how it worked. Nat even had a tattoo to remind them that the edges and peripheries were beautiful places to be.

But they hadn't even thought twice about joining in the song and dance in this tavern. They never would have done that in high society. They avoided the dance floor at all costs. Avoided attention wherever possible.

But this hadn't felt like attention. Not the peering eyes and judgement of the ton. This had felt like... Nat couldn't begin to name it.

10
Do You Have Anything To Say For Yourself?

Pinks and oranges decorated the horizon as Aleksei and Nat left the tavern. "I'm surprised," Nat admitted.

"About what?"

"That you didn't ask."

"Ask what?"

Nat smiled. "About my family name, Sunflower. I kind of expected this to just be some larger part of that whole situation."

Aleksei shook his head. "I thought about it, I should have, but..."

Nat waited, content to walk the streets of the Shenai pirate port in relative silence. The markets were still bustling, setting out lanterns coated in paper to diffuse the light. Would a pirate port ever sleep?

Nat hadn't been particularly familiar with the docks in Enderand; they had no reason to frequent them. But their time on a naval ship told them early mornings were the expectation for all ship-faring folks. Maybe Dinium was like this too. Busy in the evenings for the ton, busy in the morning for working classes. But markets in Dinium tended toward being open in the bright sunshine.

Nat hoped the working practises in Shenai Pirate Port matched the ideals they'd seen on a trodden down leaflet. Four, Eight, and Twelve. Four hours for work, eight for rest, and twelve for real life. It seemed reasonable to Nat at the time, more so now that they had actually worked on a ship. Even if they knew most of the ton wouldn't agree. They'd tried more than once to filter their opinion into the peripheries, hoping it would make a difference, only to be slapped with the long-held, foolish notion that keeping the poor busy was the only way to keep them safe. Controlled was more like it. Controlled and quiet.

Downtrodden people with no time granted to think for themselves always sought leaders. And they didn't have the time to consider whether any particular leader was what or who they wanted.

"It just didn't feel right," Aleksei said. "I've never even thought of avoiding the Captain's orders like this before. She's—" he cut himself off with a choked off gasp.

Nat looked up.

They had made it back to the dock, back to the ship. And the Captain stood at the edge of the boarding plank, cleaning under her fingernails with a dagger. Nat swallowed thickly at the silver shining blade. Their arm ached in a rhythm that matched the way the light glinted off it. They wrapped their dandified person around themself, tugging tight to the blanket of it like a child afraid of monsters under the bed. Except the monster was in front of Nat, over a rickety boarding plank. What they would give to turn tail and never have to cross that thin piece of wood.

The boarding plank rattled under their feet, filling their head with images of a sword in the hand of the pirate at their back, despite having never seen Aleksei brandish a weapon. As if this plank were not the bridge between two sturdy locations, but hanging out over the open ocean with sea-monsters or sirens writhing beneath, ready to eat Nat at the first opportunity.

The silver glint of the Captain's dagger in the orange lanterns swinging in the wind that whipped through the Shenai Pirate Port looked a little too much like scales, the flash of something not quite ready to make itself visible. Something that set the fundamental human survival instincts inside every person, even highly trained socialites, ablaze with anxiety.

Nat's heart thumped, overpoweringly loud in their ears, silencing the endless noises of a busy port — even at night. Their legs itched to run. Clinging tighter to their dandy persona they let their gentle smile stretch over their face, hips settling into a soft, gender neutral sway. Behaving as if they were any other member of the crew, able and allowed to come and go as they pleased.

"I hear you made quite the spectacle of yourselves," the Captain sneered.

"It was just a brief outing," Aleksei said, but he was folding in on himself the way so many people did when facing down someone with much more power about to reprimand them.

The way Nat did around their father.

"Secure the cash and *then* you can make your case, and take your punishment."

Thoroughly cowed by even such a simple statement, Aleksei practically scurried Nat into the cells below deck, using the keys that always rattled at his waist to lock the door behind them.

Nat turned to say something to him, some whispered words that would ease or at least clarify what was to happen from here. To understand what the Captain had meant by 'punishment'. But Aleksei was already scampering from the room.

Felitabby watched in surprising quiet.

"What?" Nat asked.

He scoffed and turned away.

Nat rolled their eyes and settled themself into the corner of their cell, back against the two wooden walls, the full expanse of the space set out before them.

They pulled their knees up to their chest and tucked their face away into them.

Punishment. The thorough telling off Aleksei was about to be subjected to. And for what? Spectacle. Scandal. All things Nat was far too uncomfortably familiar with.

They had never intended to breach the line of scandal. They had always been oh so careful to stay on the safe side of things.

Don't think about it.

Don't think about it.

Don't.

But it was futile.

Nat's ever-racing and under-stimulated brain couldn't help but draw the parallels. Couldn't help but think of the last time they had been so horribly ineffective and doomed.

*N*at gripped their cuffs tightly against their palms. Their heart thundered, battering their sternum, a cacophony in their ears. Still, they maintained as close to a neutral, detached expression as they could manage.

Their father sat, leaning back in his chair, barred from Nat by his huge ornate desk. His stomach swelled when he leaned like that, putting pressure on his waistcoat buttons. The fabric implied an evening garment despite the sun only just reaching its peak in the sky.

Light filtered through the windows behind him, highlighting the red in his hair, the feature that marked him and Nat most closely as family.

"Your actions at the ball last night," he finally said. "Do you have any explanation? Anything to say for yourself?"

Nat swallowed. They could ask what he meant. But they knew. They had snuck away to the library with Rajni. It didn't much matter what they had planned to do, nor what they had done. All that mattered was that somebody had noticed their absence, or their return, or their freshly retied cravat.

Pinpricks of red spread over their father's face as the silence stretched between them. Words rose and lodged in Nat's throat. Explanations. Excuses. Lies. But nothing came out. They had nothing to offer. What could they do? Throw themself on their father's mercy? And what might that accomplish? They both knew what he knew. An apology would be confirmation, a denial would be an insult.

"Probably best that you choose silence." Their father pushed forward in his chair, picking up a folded piece of cream coloured paper from the desk. The family crest from his signet ring stood out in stark wax, just as red as Nat's hair. "Pack your bags; I've arranged a naval apprenticeship for you. A year at sea should straighten you out."

Before Nat could protest, request, beg their father to forgive them just this once and let them stay. Before they could promise better behaviour, to never leave a chaperone's side. Before they could offer up that this was their first noticed indiscretion, the only time they'd been caught in misbehaviour and even then it was barely caught. Their father held up a hand.

He passed them the letter, his neat, simple handwriting in stark black ink on the opposite side to the seal.

Rear-Admiral Eads
HMS The Valiant

Nat pressed their lips together; turning on their heel, they fled their father's study.

The captain's cabin on this pirate ship was a spacious room, the entire back wall coated in glass that let the light shine in just a blindingly as it did on deck. A desk filled the centre of the space, sturdy, leather inlaid, and almost exactly what Rear-Admiral Eads' desk had looked like.

Nat looked away from it. They didn't need the reminder of naval men and their desks. They didn't need the reminder of Rear-Admiral Eads and his untimely death. They didn't need the reminder, painfully poking at their sleep-deprived head that they had stood in a room with a desk exactly like this at exactly half of the worst days of their life.

As if Nat wouldn't have already been filled with dread at the privacy of a pirate captain's cabin. Let alone so soon after having absconded from the ship without apparent permission to do so.

They hadn't seen Aleksei since. It was hard to catch glimpses of people when you were locked in a cell below deck, but Aleksei's absence was... notable to say the least.

In one oddly sized alcove, a wrought metal bed-frame had been tied to the wall to keep it from shifting with the waves. Wait. Were those ropes for tying it to the wall or...?

Nat decided to keep their eyes on their boots. But even those just reminded Nat of their brief naval history. How they longed for shoes that suited. Shoes that made each step the perfect accompaniment to the outfit. Shoes that were Nat's own, rather than uniform standard. Anything that was Nat's own rather than uniform standard or ill-fittingly borrowed.

"Would either of you care to give yourselves up?" the Captain asked.

"Give ourselves up?" Felitabby echoed.

"Tell me who your family is, or who the other person's family is? Make things easy for me so I don't have to take you into the bustling of the Shenai Pirate Port."

"I won't tell you anything!" Felitabby crowed.

"And you?" The Captain tilted Nat's head up with two strong fingers under their chin. "Do you have anything to say?"

More of an invitation than what had been offered to Felitabby. Not just about their family, then. Room to apologise for the previous day? Or perhaps to turn on Aleksei? Claim he took them without their permission? That he put them up to the so-called spectacle?

Nat shrugged. "I can hardly be held to a lower standard than Thomin here."

The captain laughed. It sent a chill down Nat's spine. "A shame." She returned to her desk. "If either of you wants to visit the port itself, do let me know and I'll find you a suitable guard." She looked up, meeting Nat's eye with a hard set to her face. "Not Quartermaster Zima. He won't be available for a while now."

Nat's face flushed at the insinuation, hot and uncomfortable enough that they wanted to fidget. The potential layers to a statement like that, the questions it raised. Where was he? What had she meant by punishment?

Would Nat ever see him again? The insinuation that Nat was the one manipulating with kisses and wiles in exactly the way the Captain had wanted Aleksei to attempt to do to Nat. As if Nat had ever been the kind to use wiles like that.

But none of that was helpful. None of that would get Nat what they wanted. They needed to appease this Captain enough to gain a modicum of trust, to be allowed to grasp that tiny piece of freedom the Captain was dangling in front of their face, the proverbial fruit above Tantalus' head. The ability to leave the ship, to explore the Shenai Pirate Port. What were the right words to take themself out of Tantalus' spot? How could they grasp this offer without the Captain yanking it out of their reach before their fingers even brushed against it?

They didn't have the information required. The Captain was an enigma, she never spent any time near Nat and her crew was cagey about her, all unwilling to share much information. As if they feared her. As if the control she exerted over her crew were so absolute that she would know if they said anything less than perfect about her. Just like Nat's father had been to his family.

Nat gripped tight to the cuffs of the ill-fitting shirt. Eyes on them. That would appeal. Eyes on them and the implication that it might loosen their tongue. "I would appreciate a guide, of course. Someone such as I can hardly be expected to wander about alone. Particularly in somewhere so dangerous as a port."

The glare from Felitabby could have burned Nat. They ignored it. Just because he couldn't think more than one step ahead of himself didn't mean Nat was equally foolish.

11
Poseidon's Prisoner

Slipping away from their assigned babysitter in the Shenai Pirate Port was all too easy, particularly in the densely populated marketplace. Dipping between people in the ebb and flow of a crowd's movement was fundamentally of little difference to weaving through a crowded ballroom.

The guilt was less easy to ignore. The pirate Captain would take badly to her crewman losing Nat. Especially since Nat had stuck to the first babysitter she had offered the previous day, had returned to the ship and let themself be locked back below deck after the sun had disappeared below the horizon. And on the return from their abscondment with Aleksei, Nat had been clearly walking freely. But with every day of that unrelenting heat and humidity, every day of the promise of that forewarned storm, Nat's desperation grew. No matter what, they needed to be out before the storm hit.

They had to believe she would do far worse to them. If the pirate didn't want to go back he didn't have to anyway. He could board another pirate ship if he was worried about it. This was, after all, a Pirate Port.

And the way his fingers dug into Nat's injured arm at every possible step away, at every distraction: imagined or real, was making Nat's teeth grind. They couldn't handle that kind of treatment. Couldn't stand it.

The scents of frying meat and cooking bread assaulted Nat's poor empty stomach as they disappeared into a side street. Still well populated so they wouldn't stand out too badly even in their ill-fitting borrowed clothes. Even with their distinctively red hair.

A huge palace atop a hill dragged at Nat's attention in a way that seemed entirely purposeful. They tried to ignore it. From what little they'd overheard and understood, the leader of the area, the so-called Pirate

Lord reigned from that palace. A looming presence.

Nat didn't need a Pirate Lord. Nat needed a good meal, some appropriate clothing that didn't tug at the heavily buried feeling of dysphoria, and a plan.

One particular stall they passed smelled so good it pulled Nat to a halt to inhale deeply. Fried bread, cooked meat, and more spices than Nat could name. Nat had always been partial to spicy food.

"Would you like one?" a heavily accented voice asked.

Nat sighed. "I'm a tad low on funds."

"My treat." The owner of the voice turned to face the stall owner, the short plait sitting over his shoulder shifting with the motion. The pair conversed briefly in Shenai.

He passed Nat a round, white bread bun. It was hot in Nat's hand. They inhaled the steam rising from it, revelling in the scent and the warmth and having something to eat besides the oatmeal-rice breakfasts and stale tack biscuits with unpleasant grey stew dinners that seemed to be typical ship faire.

"Everyone in a Pirate Port wants food," the Shenai man spoke again, drawing Nat out of their reverie. "That's why there are so many good stalls."

His clothes were deep green and bright gold, a perfect complement to his fawny skin and dark hair. They fit well, obviously tailored to him and well cared for. In the Shenai style with buttons along the same shoulder his plait sat on and up the short collar, rather than the Ropian style with the buttons up the front.

The shirt sat lower down his body too, not tucked into his trousers, reaching the top of his thighs. Elongating his body in a pleasant way.

His dark eyes sparkled with knowledge and interest. Assessing Nat just as surely as they assessed him, in a way that sent a thrill up Nat's spine.

They knew that look.

A dandy. A pirate dandy.

Nat bit into the bread bun, taking the time to savour the flavour and texture. Even if they hadn't been subsisting on tack biscuits and unpleasant mystery stew for months, this would have been one of the best things they ever put into their mouth.

"I haven't seen you before," the new dandy said.

"No," Nat agreed.

"I'm Tao."

"Nat."

"What ship are you with?"

Nat froze midway to another bite. Fuck. What ship were they with? They continued their aborted bite to save themself a few seconds as their mind raced. They had been on *The Valiant* but that wasn't this ship. It had been too dark when the pirates attacked, even if the sheeting rain hadn't obscured everything. Since then, Nat had only been offered the opportunity to see the side of the ship in the light once.

Even so, would they want to claim this ship if they could remember the name? Or would it be better to claim to belong to another ship? How could they get out of this Pirate Port and back home? Could they even go back home? Would their father just set them on another navy ship as soon as they turned up on the doorstep?

Nat swallowed thickly.

Tao smiled.

Nat's stomach warmed at the danger contained there in a completely different way to the thrill of talking with another dandy.

"That's fine," he said. "We can discuss that later."

"Later?"

"First let me show you around."

Nat held up a hand. Interest or not, thrilling as it would be to talk properly with a dandy after so long without, as enthralled by this particular pirate dandy as they were, they couldn't risk being spotted. The Captain would take Nat's running off far worse than their previous forbidden foray into the local tavern. "That's really okay."

But even that little was too much information to volunteer to a dandy. Tao's quick gaze tracked over Nat again, lingering at the ill-fitting shirt below the grubby white waistcoat.

Dysphoria was something with which Nat was fundamentally acquainted. It had been their solemn companion since puberty hit. They had taken steps to lessen it, to minimise the discomfort of having a body that didn't always match one's gender. But this borrowed shirt, the naval uniform, none of that provided the protection that Nat sought from clothing, and with the addition of the pain Nat was trying their hardest to ignore creating an increased awareness of their body, dysphoria was inevitable.

Tao's lingering attentions while Nat was dressed this way built that same swirling storm in their stomach that mislabelling did. When someone called Nat by the wrong title, whether not of the right status or not of the right gender. That same twisting knot of discomfort. Knowing someone saw a piece of you that didn't match the rest of what you were presenting. Knowing it would be all the more difficult to convince them to adjust that view.

"Hiding?" he asked.

Nat plastered their easy and falsified dandy smile into place. "Why would I be doing that?"

"Because you can't run."

Nat would have let out the laugh that perfectly matched their smile. Except that was when their babysitter appeared around the corner of the side street, face reddened.

It could be the heat and unrelenting humidity of Shenai had got to him. But, somehow, Nat was inclined to say it was more likely the frustration or even anger of Nat having slipped out of his grasp.

"You!" he snarled, stalking forward.

Nat stepped back. All that dandy practise disappearing under the weight of physical threat. The weight of the reminder of all that had happened since that awful day in their father's office. It wasn't that Nat disbelieved what they had said to Aleksei, ultimately people had already decided if they were going to hurt you, almost regardless of what you did. But, in this particular case, Nat had definitely triggered this pirate's ire.

Tao turned to the approaching pirate and stepped in front of Nat.

The pirate stopped, eyes blowing wise as he recognised Tao.

"*Poseidon's* then," Tao muttered. "If your Captain won't pay appropriate tribute in the appropriate time, tell her the Pirate Lord won't allow her to stay, storm or not. And he definitely won't take kindly to her failing to secure her prisoners."

Nat's shoulders slumped. Ruse gone. Dead in the water. Tao had figured it out from one short conversation interrupted by an irate pirate.

They took a step back. The *Poseidon's* crewman's attention snapped to them and Tao spun back around. The lingering vestiges of a frown shifted into the calculated interest of their earlier interaction. "Come," he invited, taking hold of Nat's hand. "You strike me as a person more suited to finer clothing than..." He trailed off with a distasteful glance as Nat's unpleasant combination.

"With an invitation like that, how could I refuse?" Nat replied with all the falsified confidence they could muster. At least it wasn't back to the ship upon which they'd been a prisoner. Apparently *Poseidon's*.

12
The Pirate Lord

The bathtub was made out of green stone. Nat couldn't begin to say what kind of stone it was, but it was green and the novelty of that was doing a fair enough job of staving off both the dysphoria and the concern about the fact that their mangled looking arm wasn't healing as well as it probably should have.

They scrubbed the salt and dirt and blood and pain off their skin as rapidly as they could. The sooner they were clean, the sooner they could be out of this bathtub and into some clothes. Hopefully clothes that wouldn't pull into abject focus all those aspects of their physical form that made Nat squirm.

On the other hand, perhaps they should stay in the bath until the water turned frigid because there was no way Nat was prepared for the situation that awaited them beyond the bathroom doors.

Tao had used his grip on Nat's hand to slip an arm around theirs. Shockingly familiar. Nat had only kept their protest in because they recognised the power imbalance in the situation. This wasn't a forward arm link, it was a capturing one. Nat's only other option being returning to the ship they had run from, they had let it be, let Tao lead them up the steeply sloped road. The relentless humidity pressed against Nat's ever fraying nerves. Their concentration pulled in too many directions to recognise their intended destination until they passed through the red, circular outer gates.

The palace stretched above them, gleaming in gold and the same bright red as Nat's hair. "We match," they had whispered.

"Indeed you do."

They hadn't mentioned their next thought. The wonder as to whether a Pirate Lord might enjoy that fact. Or resent it.

They hadn't bothered to ask why they were there. Nat wasn't a fool. Tao obviously had some connection to the Pirate Lord. A high one at that if Nat's babysitter's reaction to him was anything to judge by. Nat hadn't discarded the idea that Tao, the dandy who had bought them a steamed bun filled with well-seasoned pork was, in fact, the Pirate Lord Himself. They would have expected a Pirate Lord to be more... typically piratical than Tao had presented so far, had presumed dandies in the pirate sphere would stay on the outskirts like high society dandies did. But they weren't ruling anything out.

The dressing room matched the bathroom in its green stone stylings. Privacy screens with delicate thin paper decorated in beautiful, intricate ink paintings separated areas. Behind one, atop a stone bench, sat a pile of clothes for Nat to wear.

Once fully dressed in an outfit that only mildly didn't fit —still too broad in the shoulder, leaving sleeves with no cuffs to slide over Nat's hands— Nat pressed through the next set of doors and into a corridor where a woman waited. She pointed to a dark wood door. Nat gulped and pushed it open.

The room within matched the rest of the palace's aesthetics. All green and gold and dark woods. Two dark green velvet sofas sat facing one another; a low dark wood table squatting between them. Gold and clean-glass lanterns cast a soft glow over the room. The light gleamed on Tao's luxurious dark hair. He lounged on one of the sofas, facing away from the door through which Nat had entered.

Nat shifted around the sofa to see him. His eyes raked over them, taking in their appearance in the green Shenai style clothes that matched his so well that Nat couldn't imagine they had ever belonged to anyone else. He gestured to the seat opposite and Nat gingerly took it. The door they had entered through had disappeared into the wall. No way out.

"I must say," Tao said as a different person brought in a tray of tea things. "You do clean up nicely."

Nat wanted to preen under the compliment. Their chest swelled with it. They pushed the feeling aside. Praise had always been hard won and they wouldn't be manipulated by it. Their hair dripped into their face, a droplet landing on their nose. They swiped it away. Washing their hair had probably been foolish, it always took forever to dry, but Nat couldn't bear the thought of leaving it when this was the first opportunity they had had to be *clean* in more time than they wished to count.

"I'm sure it's entirely due to my host's excellent tastes."

Tao pursed his lips. Maybe he wasn't the Pirate Lord after all, with a reaction like that. "Tea?"

"Thank you." Nat took the delicate porcelain cup in their hand, warmth seeping into their fingers. It was cool in here. This windowless little room, a den hidden away somewhere in the bowels of the Pirate Lord's Palace.

Like everything else, the cup was in the Shenai style, no handles and decorated with the same delicate lines as the privacy screens had been. Nat inhaled the flavoured steam before sipping at the drink.

"Tell me," Tao started when Nat almost felt comfortable with the silence and the delicious scent of jasmine tea swirling in the air. "What is it about you that has the Captain of *Poseidon's* in such a state?"

"A state?" Nat laughed. "She's hardly in a state over me."

"Is that so? Then why the relative freedom? Why the personal guard?"

And why did you slip away? The question wasn't spoken but it hung in the air.

"Oh," Nat said, attempting for a casual tone. Flippant. As if this were all routine. "I believe she wishes to ransom me back to my family as she did the others."

Tao grimaced. "I never did care for ransoms."

"Unfortunately for all involved, I'm not worth much."

Tao's eyebrows crept up.

Nat swallowed. Had that been a foolish thing to say? It was the truth.

"Is that so?" Tao said eventually.

"Quite. I never was the most useful sort. You know how it is in high society." Not that Nat knew whether Tao had any kind of experience in or knowledge of high society. But easier to assume and flatter than hedge and insult. "Lieges and Mxs are always the least favoured. Then there's my dandyish ways." They let out that practised laugh. It came out brittle.

Tao's intelligent eyes sparkled but he said nothing.

Nat sipped their tea. The silence pounded against their ears. No swoosh of the sea, no clatter of people working. Such silence would have meant peace only a short while ago. They had longed for silence. But this was not a peaceful silence. And, stranded in it, Nat's thoughts raced around and around.

The conversation shifted as the food disappeared. Delicate biscuits and pastries filled with something sticky and somehow both savoury and sweet all at once. One of Tao's people appeared with more tea, disappearing without so much as a word to either of them.

Tao spoke with confidence and certainty on the things he knew. Like answering how the port could exist as part of the Unknown World.

"The magic of the world tends to sit in clusters. Between that and the sea monsters most navies won't sail around, we technically fall off the official edges of the naval maps. Pirates, particularly Coded pirates have tools and skills to sail in more dangerous waters."

Like Nat bargaining with sirens, they supposed.

It wasn't just speaking on topics he knew that made Tao appealing. He questioned with honest curiosity on the things he didn't. Always apparently more than happy to discover something new, even something so simple as how an embroidery stitch could fix a sail.

Nat was halfway through an explanation of how tight embroidery stitches needed to be when a knock came on one of the walls. With a brief response from Tao, a hidden door swung inward, revealing a pale corridor that made Nat wince at its brightness. The gas lamps in here really did foster an intimacy.

Aleksei, it turned out, cleaned up nice: a neat shirt, actually buttoned to the top for a change — not that it fit, too large around the torso. If Nat was being generous they'd label it 'old fashioned' but at least this one didn't have any obvious patching up or worn out places. Clean fitted trousers tucked into his boots and, if Nat wasn't mistaken, he had brushed his hair with something other than his fingers. One of Tao's people stood to his side, eyes fixed on the intruding pirate. Interesting that he wasn't permitted to wander alone at all when Nat had shown themself into this particular room with no more than a corridor maid-guard.

Aleksei's eyes lingered on Tao for a long time, leaving him standing in the doorway, silhouetted in the light like some kind of mirage. His throat bobbed as he swallowed. He stepped fully into the room.

Tao nodded to his escort, who dipped back out, pulling the door closed once again. Leaving Nat alone with the Pirate Lord and one of the pirates that had captured them.

Aleksei's eyes trailed over toward Nat, on the opposite sofa to Tao. They couldn't mistake the look in his eye. Desire. Tao and Aleksei had something, or had done at some point, and Aleksei still wanted it. Still wanted Tao.

Did he give up on Tao the same way he had Nat? Ruined his own chances by his loyalty to his captain?

Nat plastered on their dandy smile. "What brings you up to the Pirate Lord's Palace, Peaches?"

"Peaches?" Tao's eyebrows jerked up.

"It's just a nickname."

"Just?" Tao muttered, tone too guarded for Nat to parse. Jealousy? Protectiveness? But of whom? Nat or Aleksei? Or was he simply surprised to find someone could use nicknames so easily as Nat did. Regardless of levels of intimacy.

Tao seemed the sort to put a lot of stock in a name, or at least in what one was called.

"My Lord." Aleksei's voice turned breathy as he returned his focus to the person in the room with the most power.

"You have been gone a long while," Tao spoke in a voice as soft and smooth as caramel. He raised a hand to run soft fingers along Aleksei's jaw.

Nat gulped, resolving themself to silence and the visage of their own lap. Whatever this was, Nat probably wasn't meant to be privy to it.

Tao sighed. "So, she sent *you*." It wasn't a question. The rustling of fabric sounded. Nat risked a peek up to see Tao had stood, stepping away from the frozen and flushed Aleksei. "It's hardly appropriate."

"You and she don't get along."

Tao leaned against a wall, his shoulder cocked against it in such a similar way to how Nat had leant against the cell bars that first day on the pirate ship. Behind him, a painting swirled: a pair of ships in the midst of a battle, waves crashing up over the edges of the canvas. The pattern of the wallpaper behind the frame made it seem like the water spilled all the way onto the walls.

"That hardly matters in situations such as these, Lyosha, and you know it."

Ah. That explained the issue with Peaches. Lyosha, the Kovian diminutive of Aleksei. They were close. Which Nat had already picked up on. Close enough for diminutive names. Tao could be expected, then, it would seem, to use nicknames as an indicator of intimacy, closeness.

Not so much the case for Nat. Names themselves held so much power in high society. Only Nat's family ever really used their given name. And even then...

Bear's comment of being called 'hey, you' had been a little too familiar for Nat's liking.

"I..." Aleksei sighed, running a hand through his hair, turning it from its neat state into its usual disarray. "She wants her prize back."

"Did she at least send you with tribute?"

Aleksei looked down at his feet.

Tao laughed. "I have half a mind to demand this prize as tribute in that case."

"And what exactly would that mean?"

Tao's eyes thinned, his voice took on a dangerous tone that sent shivers up Nat's spine but created that same curious warmth in their stomach. "Would that matter? I am the Pirate Lord, after all, and this is my Port. Can I not do as I will with what I am provided? Claim what I want?"

Pirates. Nat kept forgetting— not forgetting exactly, but it slipped their mind. It was all too easy to see the civility. Mere moments ago, Nat had been sharing tea and conversation with the man now describing them as a prize to be stolen. A prize to be claimed. And this from a man Nat had told that they were unransomable. Who knew better than anyone but Nat themself, how little Nat was actually worth.

Tao shifted over to Nat, laying a hand on their shoulder. Even the light contact had Nat's heart racing in their chest. Fear. Interest. That fluttering warmth in their stomach. The illicit thrill of potential. "Tell your Captain I will keep them until she sees fit to offer me the respect I deserve in my own port."

"Tao—"

"Now," Tao interrupted. "Quartermaster Zima."

Aleksei's jaw clenched. He spun on his heel and barged out of the door through which he had entered.

"Well," Tao said, dusting imaginary dirt off his shirt. "That was unpleasant; shall we swap to happier matters?"

13
What Did You Expect?

"You are the Pirate Lord."

Tao smiled that dangerous smile. "You already knew that."

"I was mostly certain, yes, but confirmation is always useful."

"Am I not what you expected?"

"No," Nat admitted.

"And what did you expect?"

"When one hears the title Pirate Lord, one expects to find a person dripping in jewels and sporting a comically oversized hat, perhaps with some feathers hanging from it. Like something out of an operetta. You're... not that."

Tao sighed, sinking back into his spot on the sofa opposite Nat. "And now you think of me differently?"

Did they? Was he any more or less dangerous for being the Pirate Lord as opposed to one of the Pirate Lord's people? As opposed to any other random pirate? Nat examined Tao's slumped stance on the sofa. This was the man who had protected them twice over. "No."

"No?"

"I think of you no differently. You're just as dangerous as when I followed you up here. Ultimately, if you want to hurt me," that dandified smile felt brittle at the edges, like a porcelain doll with a face about to shatter, "you will. As a Pirate Lord probably should."

Tao leaned forward, closing the distance between them over the squat table. "What makes you so certain?"

"That's just how it works. People justify it, but there are lines they will cross and lines they won't. I have no control over the actions of others. If you want to hurt me, you will. My scrabbling to stay safe doesn't really change anything, except, maybe, where the lines lie." They let out a practised laugh. "But that's hardly a happier matter. What would the Pirate Lord wish to discuss?"

Tao blinked. He shifted in his seat once again, as if comfort was impossible to manage. As if the sofa beneath him had changed in the time Aleksei had been in the room.

He rose, pulling out the ships painting and retrieving a bottle of wine and two glasses. Without another word he poured himself and Nat each a generous portion.

"You and Aleksei..." Nat began slowly, teasing out the question without needing to find specific words to ask it with.

"We used to fuck."

Nat's cheeks heated, their head jerked to stare into their lap once again.

"That is what you were asking, is it not?"

"You... don't anymore"

"Not since—" he stopped. "No. Not anymore."

Since. Questions burned on Nat's tongue but they were still a liege and still a dandy, so they pushed it aside. Washing it away with a slightly too large gulp of wine. "You do those kinds of things often?"

The corner of Tao's mouth tilted into a smile. "Often is a variable word."

"Regularly? A lot?"

"There is no shame in pleasure here. I find pleasure when and where I want."

Nat licked their lips. No shame... Nat had never considered pleasure, shared pleasure, without shame and fear and secrecy. But Tao had admitted to having shared something with Aleksei like it was no big deal.

The jaunts with others in libraries and other secluded areas that Nat had enjoyed in high society had largely been part of a larger concept. An exchange of information. A power play. Pleasure was the interesting side benefit. And Nat had been under no illusions that they could easily have been replaced with a dozen stand-in dandies. Except, maybe, with Rajni. It had felt different with her. At least to Nat.

Rajni. Their almost-scandal. The person Nat had felt most strongly for. The way she spoke, the way she carried herself, the bright spark in her eye. Nat's favourite thing had always been sitting in whatever receiving room with Rajni while she explained one of her newest inventions. Their family had called her a blue stocking, fired it at Nat about her like it was the most heinous of insults.

What had happened to her after Nat had been sent to sea?

"Do you love him?" they asked.

Tao paused, as if he had never expected to be asked such a question by anyone let alone this relative stranger being used as a bargaining chip. He examined them, eyes flicking over the way Nat played with the stem of the wine glass, the way their feet shifted, not quite bouncing their knees. His dark eyes bored into Nat's. "Once," He said finally. "For a time."

Nat nodded slowly. They pressed their fingers into the stem of the wine glass hard enough that the liquid left inside trembled and rippled with it. Nat wasn't meant for things like that. Affection. Care. Love. They didn't even have the capacity for it, they thought. Not even with Rajni. Nat knew better than to hope for that.

One day, Nat would have to marry. And only the poor married for love. For the ton, marriage was business. Nat was a difficult enough prospect with both the burden and benefit of their father's assets on their shoulders. Nat was the elder child and their sister couldn't inherit anyway. If Nat didn't make it back home, all their family assets would have to go to whomsoever their sister married.

"So many thoughts, Dandy." The new nickname startled Nat out of their spiral. They looked up at Tao, intent as ever. Those eyes that saw everything. No wonder he was the Pirate Lord. "Do you care to share any of them?"

"I'm not jealous."

"Usually said by the jealous."

A little laugh escaped them, a real one shocked out by the teasing. "No. Aleksei and I were almost..." They shook their head. "I was just considering the differences."

"I didn't think high society types went in for that."

Nat pouted for effect. "Are you going to tell on me?"

Tao blinked.

Nat laughed. "You'd have to find out my family name first and I'm hardly about to own that after everything I've been through."

"Oh?"

Nat shook their head. "I'm sure it's nothing to a pirate."

Tao sipped his wine, his eyes never leaving Nat, pinning them to their spot. "Tell me, Dandy, would Aleksei have been your first?"

Nat snorted. "Sorry. My apologies." They pressed gentle fingers against their mouth to try and keep from laughing too hard at the Pirate Lord. "He very much would not have been."

Tao tilted his head, his lips shifting into a soft smile. "You are not what I expected."

"And what did you expect?"

14
My Most Sincere Apologies

"My Lord, the Captain of *Poseidon's* is in the throne room."

It had been another piece of conversation interrupted with a quiet knock, from the wall opposite the painting of ships. Tao had pushed up from the sofa and tugged another hidden door open only enough to allow those words in.

Throne room. Quite the title.

Tao turned from the doorway and offered Nat a smile that hid more things than it showed.

Nat set their wine glass down on the squat table, the red residue reminding them of blood and the deepest depths of the sea. Homer's wine dark sea filled with monsters and danger. Were they more of an Odysseus, doomed to wander the world for many years before returning home? Or worse still, one of his crew, destined only to die?

"Would you accompany me to the throne room?" Tao asked, tugging the door all the way open, as if it were an ordinary invitation. As if it weren't signing their own prison order. But Nat was all too familiar with being compliant in their downfall.

They dipped under his arm holding the door open and into yet another corridor.

Trailing after Tao through his palace, Nat kept their eyes trained on the back of his shirt. Their legs felt like lead, heavy and difficult to move and leeching out poison into the rest of them.

They did not want to be returned to the custody of the pirate Captain. They would rather have remained a prize of the Pirate Lord. At least he had *some* kind of manners. But there she stood in the centre of the room. Out of place amongst the cream coloured walls, next to the jade green platform in the centre atop which a huge wooden chair perched, cushioned and draped in greens and golds.

Tension rippled over the room, heavy as the humidity, as Tao stepped aside to reveal Nat behind him. Draped in his style and colours. "As you can see, Captain," he began.

"I haven't done anything untoward with our friend here. Unless you count replacing their truly heinous outfiture."

"Here." The Captain held out a wrapped package.

Tao raised an eyebrow. "And what is that?"

"Your tribute."

"And my apology?"

The Captain gritted her teeth. "My most sincere apologies, Pirate Lord," she ground out.

"For...?" Tao prompted.

"For not providing you the appropriate tribute in a timely manner. And for not properly securing my prisoners when I brought them into your port." Her eyes bore into Nat. "It will not happen again."

Nat didn't mean to take a step back, but their navy uniform boots clicked quietly on the stone floor.

Tao spared them the briefest glance, his face entirely closed. Neutral.

Nat affixed their dandy smile into place. Evidently it was time for everyone to wear their masks.

The Captain returned her attention to the Pirate Lord. "I hope you will allow my ship to remain and wait out the storm."

"I would hardly force you to sail out into a storm, Captain. That would be tantamount to murder." His voice took on a cold quality, the one that had sent a frisson down Nat's spine. They should not want to hear that tone directed at them. What was wrong with them? "But know that you are on borrowed time here. When the skies clear up, I expect you to leave at the earliest opportunity."

"Believe me; I don't *want* to be here anymore than you want me to be."

"At least we can agree on one thing."

The Captain held her hand out toward Nat. "Now, are you going to allow me to leave with my walking cash?"

Tao pressed his mouth closed and stepped away from Nat.

Their heart sank. They should have known better than to put any faith in the protection of anyone, let alone a Pirate Lord. His pleasantries and manners were probably all just a concocted scheme to turn Nat against the Captain, as if that needed assistance.

They should have known better. They had told him, out and out, that they were unransomable. Why would he have any reason to keep them around?

The walk back to the ship was painfully quiet. The Captain kept her hand wrapped around Nat's arm, pressing into the painful line of wounds that decorated their skin. It burned almost as badly as the shame and fear swirling around inside them.

The humidity of the port seeped through Nat's shirt. Sweat slicked their skin.

The sun had well past set, leaving Nat stumbling over the uneven pathway. But they didn't fight. Didn't pull against the grip on them. Didn't try to separate themself from the situation. This wasn't going to end well for them. Returning to the ship was a bad idea, but what else could Nat do?

All that work they'd put into earning trust was ruined now. It wouldn't be so easy to get away again. Nor would it likely function to claim to want to stay, to tease their way back into a level of trust.

If they got out again, Nat wouldn't stop for the world. Wouldn't stop for anything less than guaranteed freedom. Certainly wouldn't stop for a vague interest in the dandy Pirate Lord.

But they doubted they would get the opportunity. The real question was whether Nat would live through the fallout from this attempt at all. Aleksei had warned that the Captain didn't hold love for those who proved to have no purpose. Nat could only imagine it would be worse for people whose purpose turned out to be pestering disobedience.

The ship came into view, standing tall and proud against the dark sea beyond. Clouds swirled in the sky, blue and green and grey. The wind whipped at the orange pinpricks of lanterns on deck.

The Captain shoved Nat up the boarding plank, the wood clattering under both their feet. Nat almost considered dropping off the edge and into the murky waters below. There wouldn't be any sea monsters to eat them inside a port, though, and drowning didn't seem a nice way to go. Plus, with Nat's luck this far, the Captain would probably just fish them out and lock them away wet with sea water.

She dragged them all the way down to the cells.

Felitabby was already locked away, leaning against the wall that marked the edge of the room. One leg extended, the other bent at the knee with his elbow resting atop it. He glanced up at Nat's violent entrance.

The Captain stuffed Nat into the cell next to him, still stained with Mr Awthorn's blood. The lock clanged shut.

"What the fuck were you thinking?" she demanded. Nat opened their mouth but before they could speak she continued, "Going to the Pirate Lord like that! Never mind the fact that you ran away from Grigg. That I could almost forgive. But the *Pirate Lord*. What the fuck were you thinking?"

Her hands were wrapped in white knuckled fists around the bars, almost as if she was the one locked away instead of Nat. As if she wanted to rip the barrier away to gain her freedom. Her face was twisted with rage. She was going to hurt Nat. It didn't matter what Nat did. And that inevitability, the hopelessness that clung to Nat because of it, it twisted inside Nat. Their face twisted into the most extreme of their dandified smiles. The let their words out, dripping with all the venom they could muster. "My most sincere apologies."

The Captain snarled and stalked off.

15
Clean That Up

Felitabby hadn't retied his ponytail, yet more hair loose around his face. He was a mess. Had Nat looked that much of a mess before the Pirate Lord had allowed them use of his bath? He surged to his feet, slamming his palm against the bars separating them. Metal clanged and rattled. "What the fuck is wrong with you?"

Nat spun to face him. "What's wrong with me? I am trying to survive this. I am not the one foolish enough to forget about mutually assured destruction. I am not the one so thoroughly wrapped up in his own superiority complex that I can't recognise when an alliance might be valuable, even if I personally find the prospect or the people within it distasteful at best."

"Mutually assured destruction?"

"I sell you out and you sell me out in turn."

"Why are you so obsessed with not being ransomed? Your family is perfectly fine! If you're only staying here out of some misguided loyalty to me or—"

"Get over yourself, Thomin. This has nothing to do with you. I quite literally just tried to escape alone. I cannot be ransomed back, okay? It doesn't matter why. What matters is that it isn't a possibility for me. I have to come up with some kind of a plan and your attitude isn't helping *anything*."

"My attitude?"

"Yes, Thomin, your attitude. You and I both know I didn't want to join the navy ship in the first place. I don't want to be here either. I thought I had made that clear by now."

"You snuck out with a pirate! You wandered off with two different ones."

"I ran away. Just because I failed my attempt doesn't mean I didn't try one. How wrapped up inside your own head are you to not realise this is our best chance? This is the moment we need to seize."

"It's a Pirate Port. Where would we go from here?"

"Anywhere. We get onto another ship, we take a carriage, we walk for a thousand miles to the next nearest village and go from there. The point is to not stay prisoners, and figure it out from there. We're not going to hang around in a port like this again. We're only here for the storm. And we need to get out before it hits."

To Nat's surprise, they were permitted exit from the cell the next morning. The boarding plank had been retracted, preventing anyone from leaving the ship but there it sat, next to the bear-man. Easy enough to push over but only if Bear would allow it.

Nat followed their guards of the day— two this time —to their regular spot by the secured barrels. The piles of clothes for mending seemed to have grown in the brief time Nat had been ashore. Maybe the Captain had ripped up shirts in a fit of pique.

They settled into a position of relative comfort on the floor, picking up the mending supplies. Their fingers trembled.

Bear shifted to sit atop one of the secured barrels, in Aleksei's usual perch. Still close enough to guard the boarding ramp as well as Nat. He was radiant in his new cravat that had used to be Nat's. Nat couldn't blame or hate him for it. Not only had they given it freely, but they had never much cared for cravats. They trailed fingers over the Shenai style collar.

"You're a lot less intimidating with that," Nat teased.

Bear rolled his eyes, pressing a whetstone against the edge of his sword.

"On the other hand..."

Stitching slowly, Nat watched the crew go about their business. The shift and movement reminded them of high society dancers. Nobody ever collided, each shifting around each other in beautiful motion. But the tension of the incoming storm rippled over the top of it like a heat wave. Nat wouldn't have been able to tell the storm was coming without having heard the Captain discussing it all those days ago. They'd have noticed the tension and wouldn't have been able to puzzle out its cause. Even feeling the press of the humidity against their skin.

None of these pirates wanted to stay here. Not for the length of a tropical storm. And, from what Nat had seen in Tao's palace, they weren't wanted here either. The same kind of tension that had lingered in Nat's home when they had been sent to sea but before they had actually left. The days it had taken for Nat to pack what little they were allowed to take aboard a naval ship — all lost to them now. The tension that had lingered that evening at the dinner just contained in the family home, avoiding the event of the night. That tension seemed to follow Nat, as yet, unwilling to break.

Across the deck, Felitabby stepped up to the captain. He towered over her small stature in the same kind of way he and

Rodgerson had done to Nat. Not that Nat was especially short, not like the pirate Captain.

Nat had accepted it when Felitabby had tried it with them. Like everything else, they'd let it slide off them as best they could. It had been the least of their worries. And anyway, Rear-Admiral Eads had obviously favoured Felitabby, thanks to Thomin's friendship with Rodgerson. Rear-Admiral Eads had been Rodgerson's mentor. There had been nowhere for Nat to go, no way for them to fight back.

But the Captain was the most powerful person on this pirate ship. And her crew had proven themselves to have complete and thoughtless loyalty. What exactly did he expect to achieve? Pissing off a pirate captain had been on Nat's 'avoid if at all possible' list right up until it had happened anyway.

The bustle of the Pirate Port at Nat's back and the rhythmic rasp of Bear's whetstone covered the conversation between Felitabby and the Captain. Though conversation seemed too gentle a term for the way they interacted.

That tension roiled.

Nat's hands stilled in their stitching. Lightness invaded their chest. As if a balloon were being inflated inside their ribcage. Or a hot air balloon was heating and ready to take off and carry Nat with it.

The Captain settled back on her feet. Looked around at her surrounding crew with incredulity.

Bear's whetstone paused.

Nat glanced up to find he had turned away from the interaction. His jaw stood out sharply as his teeth clenched tight. He watched the port at Nat's back.

Nat looked back at Felitabby and the Captain.

The tension snapped.

Her sword glinted in the sunlight, shifting so fast Nat could barely register it.

Nat had seen violence. Parents who thought slapping their children was a way to make them behave, boxing, even a few naval fights in the brief time they'd been aboard *The Valiant.* But this... this was beyond anything Nat could have prepared for.

Felitabby's body slumped to the floor, as if his entire skeleton had been torn out by the sword's retreat. Bright red blood pooled around him.

The pirate Captain stepped back to avoid getting it on her boots.

She held out a hand in Aleksei's direction, not bothering to look as he deposited a cloth into it. She wiped her blade clean, dropped the cloth into the pool of blood, and started toward her regular spot at the front of the ship. This time, Nat could hear her words, called out with the intent to carry but with such a casual tone that Nat could hardly reconcile them, hardly recognise them as words at all. "Clean that up."

Bile rose up in Nat's throat. They lurched to their feet and vomited over the side of the ship.

The sound of Bear's whetstone resumed as Nat panted into the ocean.

16
Step Five

The silence that filled the cells pressed against Nat's ears. No more of Felitabby's posturing, or screaming, or even snoring. Nat was the last one left and they had seen in vivid, nauseating detail what would happen if the captain decided they were no longer more useful than they were annoying.

It shouldn't be a surprise. Aleksei had warned them all as much that first day in the cells. *If you are of no use, the Captain may not see fit to keep you around.*

Maybe Nat should just give in. Tell the Captain their family name and hope these pirates made enough of a fuss with their ransom demands that their father had little recourse but to send the full asking price.

But that was a fantasy of the highest order. There was no circumstance, no fuss large enough that Nat being held hostage, that Nat's continued absence from their family home would be anything less than a relief for their father. After all, he had sent them away for a reason. And if he chose not to pay, Nat would be no better off than they were now. If he actively refused to pay, sent a letter to clarify his stance, Nat would be just as dead as Felitabby.

And anyway, the risk that these pirates would recognise Nat's family name for its long, proud, naval history was too great. If this pirate Captain had ever had a run in with Nat's father, she'd kill Nat on the spot for their surname alone. Any pirate with links to Nat's family would.

No. The risks were too high.

Nat would just have to figure out another way to stay on the Captain's good side. A way to get back to neutral at the very least.

Step one: no more Tao. No thinking about him. No wanting to see him. No comparing the situation, food, or anything else aboard to what Tao had provided in his palace. He was a bright and shiny thing Nat couldn't afford to be distracted by.

Step two: sit in their little corner on the ship and mend. Rebuild the trust they'd so hard won and so immediately lost.

Step three: try not to vomit when they saw the staining on the deck from Felitabby's blood.

Step four: never close their eyes again lest they see the flash of reddened sword and

Felitabby's lifeless body slump to the ground.

He had made Nat's life on *The Valiant* hellish. He'd been a colossal asshole. But he had been the only person on the ship who was in something akin to the same position as Nat.

The loneliness pressed against them on all sides, making their skin itch, making them long to replace its emptiness with the warmth of skin on skin. To find what little tiny pleasure and relief could be found from such things.

They leaned their head back against the wooden wall of the cell. The lone lantern hanging in the doorway swung with the gentle movement of even the docked ship, illuminating the three empty cells between Nat and the doorway thanks to Bear escorting them back to what Nat considered their own cell.

Before being sent to sea, Nat had seen exactly one dead body: their mother. She had lain in bed, calm and peaceful, easy enough to mistake for sleeping if one didn't happen to notice the uncomfortable stillness of her. Now that count had gone up by two. And both in stunningly violent detail.

Nat pressed the heels of their hands against their eyes, hard enough that it began to hurt. As if they could press out the image of a bloodied blade. They dragged their hands down their face. There had to be something. Some way out of this mess.

Some solution. Nat just had to come up with it.

In the light, Aleksei appeared, carrying a tray with two bowls and two tankards set atop it.

Nat's stomach roiled again. They pressed a hand to their mouth.

Aleksei sat on the opposite side of the bars, back pressed up against the wood, matching Nat's position. He passed one tankard and one bowl of grey mush through to them, keeping the other for himself.

Nat ignored the food for now. Couldn't bring themself to stomach even the idea of it, let alone try to ingest it.

Aleksei began to speak, words washing over Nat. They leaned their head back against the wooden wall and tried to keep the tears clogging their throat contained.

"And she never listens to me!" Aleksei ranted. "I'm supposed to be her second in command but you wouldn't know it."

The way he had passed that cloth over, like it was a practised move repeated more times than either party cared to count, told a very different story.

"If it bothers you so much, why not leave?" Nat asked, words coming out weirdly sluggish.

"I have been with this ship longer than she has been Captain," Aleksei retorted, indignant.

Nat sighed. It was nice that Aleksei had come down, nicer still that there was someone to fill the awful, painful silence of the cells. But now he was looking for answers, looking to Nat as if they had any greater knowledge of pirate affairs. "I don't know, pick a new Captain?"

"You're suggesting a mutiny?"

Nat held their hands up. "All I'm saying is, if you're unhappy here, why not try to make a change?"

Aleksei hummed.

"You could be Captain."

"That's not how this works."

"How is that not how this works? You're second in command, right?"

"Right."

"So, if the Captain is... indisposed, you'd be in charge."

"Only if she were coming back. If she were ousted— or left of her own volition, there would have to be a vote."

Nat raised their eyebrows. "Never took pirates for the democratic sort."

Aleksei shrugged. "We live outside the bounds of society; you think that means we don't have our own rules?"

Nat shifted, crossing their legs beneath them and setting their hands to rest gently between the bars of the cells. Leaning close to Aleksei, they whispered, "Then use your rules to your own advantage. We both know your current Captain does."

"I can't do that."

"Why not?"

"It would make me a bad second." Aleksei tugged the mostly full bowl back out under the bars, leaving Nat's tankard where it was. "I should go back to deck."

"Aleksei, wait—"

He didn't. Retreating from the cells with the tray.

Nat leaned back against the wall once again, tilting their head until it rested on the wooden wall. They shut their eyes. "Step five:" they whispered to themself. "Do not forget, no matter how close you might feel to these pirates, you are fundamentally a prisoner and a meal ticket. They are beholden to their Captain above, beyond, and outside all else."

They let out a long, slow breath.

Just like the crew on *The Valiant* had been to Rear-Admiral Eads. Just like each family was supposed to be to their father.

And there was Nat, as ever, on the outside. Locked away from such connections. Inescapably too much to ever be able to join a community like that. Nat sucked at following and nobody ever wanted to follow them.

17
Tell Me, Who Should I Punish?

It took days before Nat was permitted exit from their cell again. The humidity of the coming storm had seeped into the bowels of the ship, pressing against Nat's fraying nerves. Being left alone for so long was never going to have been a good thing for Nat. Not with the way their brain spiralled and circled. Imagining various courses of action they could take or could have taken, remembering all those things that they had no business thinking about; locked in the horror of the situation they were already in.

One pirate after another had appeared, bringing offerings of more of that same grey mush and water made bitter with purifying alcohol. They dropped off the bowls, taking them away again only when the next meal appeared. Aleksei didn't reappear. No Jay or even Bear. Nat tried their best to keep their strength up, but their sleep was broken by nightmares of what happened to Felitabby, of red blood spilling over naval uniforms. The stain in Mr Awthorn's cell seemed to grow with every passing hour.

Their failed babysitter entered the room, keys jangling in his white-knuckled fist. He unlocked the door and grabbed Nat's arm, yanking them into the murky, clouded sunlight of the deck.

The Captain waited, leaning against the bow of the ship, cleaning under her fingernails with her dagger. "So," she started. "Grigg here tells me you are the one at fault for his failure to keep an eye on you and therefore my need to offer the Pirate Lord more than his fair share of tribute. What do you have to say for yourself?"

Nat glanced at Grigg, his hand still biting into their arm. "He would see things that way."

The Captain laughed. "Explain your logic."

"From his perspective, I slipped away and therefore it's my fault."

"And from another perspective?"

"From another perspective, he got distracted by satay chicken." The words dripped with snark.

The Captain laughed again.

Nat almost thought the conversation over, but for the way Grigg's fingers tightened even more. Not that they were foolish enough to truly believe it would be that easy. And, as the Captain sobered, Nat recognised a conversation well beyond their skill set, dandy or not.

"In that case, Nat." The way she said Nat's name held more weight than Nat cared for. The layers of meaning behind its use weighed at them, tugging them down. The impropriety of a first name. The intimacy of it. The knowledge that their family name must be kept secret. The idea that she might have found out anyway. "Tell me, who should I punish? You?" She pointed with the dagger. "Or him?"

Nat swallowed thickly. They could protect themself. They should. They should at least try. But Nat had never been ruthless. Had never been the kind to throw someone else in harm's way for their own protection. "It depends on your own interpretation."

"Does it?"

"Yes." They took a deep breath. Maybe they could still talk their way out of this? Save themself and Grigg all at once. "Who is more at fault in a situation where a prisoner took a chance to run at the guard's distraction? The prisoner or the guard? Is there any blame to be laid on the shoulders of the person feeding Grigg so poorly that he was able to be distracted by satay chicken?"

"You see yourself as a prisoner?"

Nat let out a bitter little laugh. "I sleep in a cell, how could I not?"

The Captain leaned forward, her breath washing over Nat's face. She smelled like the rum that sanitized the gathered rainwater into drinkable quality. Too strong to be drinking it watered down. "Would you like to be a true part of the crew?"

"I didn't imagine that would be an option."

"Because?"

"Because you think I am more valuable in coin than in skills."

"Do I?"

"Yes."

"You say that like there isn't another option."

"If you didn't, you wouldn't have given the Pirate Lord anything for my return. Not even your or Aleksei's time."

She may not know Nat's family name, but she certainly recognised that their family was well off. Whether someone on *The Valiant* had sold them out the way Nat predicted, whether just by Nat's manner the same way Tao had discerned, or by some other means, she knew it. And she wanted what she felt she was owed by keeping Nat alive. Especially after cheating herself out of Felitabby's ransom.

The Captain clapped her hands together. "I've decided."

Nat blinked, trying to catch up.

"You're both at fault and you'll both take punishment."

Nat tried to back away, an instinctive movement that got them exactly nowhere in Grigg's bruising grip.

"Captain," he protested.

"Are you disagreeing with me, Grigg?" The words came like a slap.

"No, Captain."

"Then prepare yourself to exact your punishment."

"Exact?" Nat echoed.

"Exact," the Captain repeated. "We do things particularly here. If a crew member is wronged, they are the one to choose and exact punishment. You wronged Grigg, so he punishes you. Grigg wronged me, so I punish him."

"Would you choose one to take a punishment for the rest?" the pirate captain purred at Rear-Admiral Eads.

Nat tried to wrench their arm out of Grigg's grip. But it was futile. They weren't strong. They weren't a pirate. And they were completely at Grigg's mercy.

The captain offered Grigg a braided whip and, once again, Nat wrestled for freedom. Shit. Fuck. They had to get away.

The cold splash of rain dropped onto Nat's face. It pattered down onto the deck as

Grigg secured Nat's hands to one of the endless number of railings all over the ship.

It didn't matter how hard Nat fought it. It didn't matter what Nat did.

Ultimately these people had already decided they were going to hurt Nat.

Ultimately these people had already hurt Nat on that night of capture. The night Nat had been fighting every single day not to remember, not to relive, not to think about.

The way blood had spurted from Rear-Admiral Eads's neck. His clean white shirt turning red. His clean white waistcoat slowly beginning to match. The lapels of his jacket. All from the Captain's dagger. The same one she still held as she watched Grigg raise the whip she had offered him.

On the main deck, Bear met Nat's eyes. The same bear-man who had scooped Nat up by the scruff of their neck. Now wearing the very same cravat that he had unintentionally choked them with. He winced and turned away, staring out to sea. Refusing to look at the pain the same way he had refused to look at Felitabby's death.

Aleksei, kind, caring, friendly Aleksei stood by the main mast. His jaw stood out stark just as it had that first night. As it had when he held Nat's discarded jacket while the rain lashed down on them all and Nat suffered the abuse the Captain had demanded, metered out by one of the very crew with whom Nat had been serving for months.

All the pirates here, the nicer ones and the crueller ones had seen what Nat had been subjected to, had seen what Nat's supposed Commander had done. And they had all pretended it had never come to pass, just as intent on that pretence as Nat had been.

Aleksei's head jerked down as the first lash came.

18

I Aim To Please

As the rain started in earnest, cold droplets stinging against Nat's newly exposed and raw back, the Captain turned her attention to Grigg.

Nat stumbled closer to the railing they were tied to, scrabbling at the knots with their hands and teeth, uncaring about propriety for the first time in their life. So what if these pirates thought Nat foolish or improper for biting at rope, Nat was most of the way exposed from their shirt and these pirates had just watched them be abused for the second time in mere months. They could all take it. Even so, tears streamed from their eyes, mixing with the rain water on their face.

A hand appeared as if from nowhere, untying the ropes with deft, strong fingers.

The rigger. With nary a word, they disappeared back up the rigging as if they had never been near Nat all as the rope around their wrists fell to the floor.

Another quick glance at the captain and Grigg told Nat that she was just as distracted with this as Grigg had been with the satay chicken. Nobody else looked, all settled into their tasks and, like Bear and Aleksei, purposefully turned away.

Nat hefted the boarding plank, shoving it from where it had been pushed up against the main mast. It was heavy, too much for their abused body to muster. They shoved it some kind of into place, stumbling down it with little care for its slippery nature, hopping the gap at the end as the plank splashed into the water below. Falling into the ocean didn't seem so bad now.

As the rain shifted from a slow, lazy splatter to a heavy downpour, Nat stumbled through the empty streets. They had to get somewhere. Somewhere the Captain wouldn't come looking for them. In the haze of pain and desperation, Nat crashed into the edges of buildings. Mud splattered up their legs from the sodden ground. They ricocheted off one and into a person.

"Sorry," they offered, haphazardly, reaching out for the side of a building to steady themself.

"Shit, Nat?" Tao's voice cut through the deafening panic. His hands landed softly on Nat's left arm.

They yelped, flinching away from the contact.

"Come on," he insisted.

Nat stumbled back, shaking their head. They couldn't go with Tao again. Couldn't risk him returning them to that ship. They needed to find somewhere to lay low, somewhere to wait out the storm. Then they could find a way home.

"Nat?" Rain dripped from Tao's hair into his eyes. He squinted through it. "Please. There's nowhere else you can go. Everything is closing for the storm. You need to get inside."

"Then why are you—" A peal of thunder cut them off. "Why are you out here?" they shouted over the ever increasing pounding of rain.

"Final checks. Now come on." He grabbed their hand, skin slippery in the rain water.

This time Nat wasn't alone in the room with the green bathtub. Which was probably a good thing the way the world was swirling around them, vision still invaded with sheeting rain even with a solid roof over their head. Tao sat them on one of the benches at the edge of the room. He pulled a dagger from somewhere on his person. Nat flinched away from the blade.

"I need to get that shirt off."

Nat offered a trembling nod, closing their eyes as Tao cut away the fabric, careful not to catch Nat with the blade.

"I'm going to treat—" He swore in Shenai as he found the aged and now soaking bandages spanning most of Nat's left arm. "Okay," he breathed. "I'm going to treat your injuries. It might hurt but just..."

Tao's hands pressed firmly into Nat's skin. Their breath hissed out between their teeth. Tao murmured something in Shenai as he continued his attentions.

Nat examined the delicate painted panel on the wall. Trees and birds Nat wasn't familiar with, all done out in Tao's signature colours. The images blurred as Nat's eyes narrowed in a wince.

Their mouth was moving. They were sure of it. Talking, presumably. But they couldn't quite figure out what they were saying. They should shut up. Talking with no protection, no aims, was the best way to end up in trouble. Well, aside from sneaking into somebody else's library for a secret tryst. Which was really the cause of every single subsequent piece of trouble.

When Tao was done, Nat murmured, "It's one way to ruin a shirt."

Tao let out a soft hum.

"Couldn't help myself," Nat babbled. "Desperate to see you again. Had to get myself hurt to manage it."

"You need to rest. Come."

"Bossy," Nat teased. Their head swam as they pushed to their feet to follow Tao.

The Pirate Lord grabbed their waist to keep them from falling over even as he slipped a silk robe around their shoulders to cover their torso.

"Just because you're a Lord doesn't mean you get to order me around. You're not the only one with a title here, you know."

Tao said nothing as he led Nat down a short corridor and into a bedroom. He settled them into a luxurious bed, the softest they had had in almost a year.

Nat curled up on their uninjured side under the blankets as Tao left them alone.

For one brief, blissful second, Nat almost thought they were back home. Back in their soft, warm bed waiting for their valet-maid Souris to come and officially wake them with their secret extra morning tea.

Then the pain settled over them.

Nat snuggled deeper into the bedding, ignoring the way the movement hurt.

Maybe if they hid here long enough, everything else would go away. At least hiding here meant they could avoid dealing with the fallout of the previous day.

Tao wouldn't keep them here, as proven by their last visit. He, like everyone else in pirate society, seemed to be out for only his own interests. Nat had never been good at that. Never been good at selfish. Too concerned with the status of their family, with the happiness of those they cared about; with offering what others wanted to try and keep their attention in the best way Nat knew how.

A brief knock was all the warning Nat got that someone was about to enter the room. They pushed up in the bed, wincing at all the different pains that called for their attention.

The thundering of continued rain battered against the roof and walls.

Tao entered the room, all cautious movements. He flicked the lights on, casting a warm orange glow over the space.

Nat pulled the disturbed robe closer around themself, wishing they had had a chance to rise from the bed before Tao let himself in. It had been one thing for him to treat their injuries in a bathroom, and it was one thing to share intimate forays in libraries or receiving rooms or that one time on a balcony, but none of that was sitting half-naked in a bed with a Pirate Lord assessing with his dandy-smart attention.

"May I check your injuries?"

Nat nodded and shifted where they sat, not quite ready to stand for all they wished that they had. When he was in position, they let the robe drop from around their shoulders, tucking it close to their chest.

His fingers were soft but purposeful on Nat's skin as he examined his handiwork from the previous day, of which Nat had some semblance of jumbled memory. He pressed gently against their back, slid bandages off their arm, tutting at what he found there.

Nat took measured breaths. The intimacy pressed at them. They hadn't been shirtless in front of anyone since... Possibly ever. Or at least as long as Nat could remember. Certainly never as an adult.

"My dear Dandy," Tao's voice was laden with meaning Nat couldn't quite parse out as exposed and exhausted as they were. "I do believe your face has stolen all the blood that should be attempting to heal your wounds."

With a thick swallow, Nat yanked their dandified persona around them as tightly as a poorly laced corset and twice as painful. "Perhaps that is why I am no longer bleeding."

Tao's fingers were soft as he turned Nat's face to his. "May I ask a boon? Only if you agree."

Nat nodded slowly, at least wanting to hear with Tao would ask for. What could a Pirate Lord possibly want from them?

Tao leaned close, his warm breath tickling over Nat's chin and lips, further inflaming their face. "A kiss."

Nat wanted to tease, to joke about Tao coming straight out of a romance serial with a line like that. *The Dandy and The Pirate Lord* or maybe *The Pirate Lord and The Dandy*.

Instead, they nodded.

Tao's lips were firmer than Aleksei's first kiss had been. More purposeful. And how many pirates did Nat intend to kiss exactly?

His fingers remained where they were, a soft pressure on Nat's jawline, keeping them tethered in place as his lips pressed and melded and set Nat's heart thundering in their chest and ears, and fireworks exploding in Nat's stomach.

This was unlike any kiss they had had before. And not just because they were sat in vicinity of a bed. Tao was obviously experienced, he knew what he wanted and he took it without hesitation.

Nat shifted to better press their lips to Tao's, turning in the bed to face him.

His teeth grazed Nat's lower lip and they gasped into his mouth.

Their hands flashed out to sink into Tao's hair, easily undoing the tie that kept it in its plait. It was soft and luxurious to touch. Nothing like the pomaded dos of high society, or the salt-toughened strands of Aleksei's. Tao let out a little groan as Nat's fingernails raked against his scalp.

The noise sent a flutter up Nat's spine. They wanted him to do that again.

He pulled back just enough to fan hot breath over Nat's face as he asked. "Do you know how this works?"

Nat let out a breathy laugh. "You already know this isn't my first foray into intimacy, Pirate Lord, no matter what people think about high society."

Tao's eyes were serious. Dark, intent, and oh so serious that it made Nat want to hide. And yet they never wanted him to stop looking at them like that. They wanted to squirm but they had too much decorum for such indulgences. "What experience do you have exactly? I want to know your baseline expectations before I even contemplate going further."

Nat scowled. "Are you always this delicate?"

"These discussions are important, how else will we ensure everyone involved enjoys themself?"

Nat had never given it much thought. It had always seemed to go so naturally. Instinctively. They weren't opposed to the idea of giving feedback in the moment. 'Not there.' 'Not like that.' 'Try this instead.' But that was as far as discussion went.

"I've had plenty of experiences with plenty of people."

"Details, Nat. If your experiences were a little hand action under the table—" Under a table? "— That is one thing and it re-frames the possibilities of what we could do here."

The fireworks that had been exploding in Nat's stomach dropped like anchors. Nat tugged up the semi-discarded robe to regain some semblance of modesty, some barrier between themself and Tao. He was fully dressed, in his own domain, and speaking with more authority on the topic than Nat had known was available. And Nat was ashamed. They were too experienced for the likes of high society and yet not experienced enough for the pirate in front of them. Too much and yet not enough. As always. "More than fumbling hands," they muttered.

"A bed?"

They shook their head. It had always been pushed up against windows and bookshelves and walls. And that one memorable time on a balcony balustrade. Never discarding much clothing, just shifting what was needed to make the most impact. A flush of arousal and shame rocketed through Nat in such quick success that they might as well have been interlinked.

"I see," Tao mused, obviously reacting to something in Nat's face or posture. Something Nat hadn't even been aware of.

"You got your kiss, Peaches," Nat threw the name at Tao like a dagger. "That was all you requested."

Tao stood, retreating to lean back against the wall. "If that is all you desire then I won't push. But you should know, Dandy." He fired the title back with just as much force.

Nat flushed even as their stomach clenched with wanting. They wanted him to say it again. Just like that. The way he spoke the word with interest and passion and respect even when using it as a weapon. They wanted him to press them into positions they weren't sure they were comfortable with and call them Dandy like it was a word just for them. "Things are different amongst pirates."

"I had noticed that much on my own."

"Like I said, pleasure is not shameful here. But with that comes a lack of permanence. We find pleasure and we let it go."

"I'm not clingy," Nat defended. Secret trysts hardly made for committed relationships.

Tao raised one eyebrow, mouth quirking up at the corners. "Perhaps not, but I wonder how true that would be after more than you'd ever experienced before."

"Is that what you claim to be offering, Princess?"

"Princess?"

"You live up here in your fancy palace and claim you know all that happens below you. Princess." For the briefest instant, Nat thought they had gone too far.

Then Tao laughed. "You are cutting when you want to be."

The compliment took Nat off balance. They laid a hand on the bed to steady themself under the weight of it. They offered Tao a smile and it felt a little dangerous. "I aim to please."

Tao laughed again. "I'll bet you do."

19
I Like To Play With Dangerous Things

Tao handed over a small, folded pile of clothes: a sage coloured silk shirt with top-to-bottom buttons down the front, the type Nat was more used to, sat on top of the pile. They turned away from Tao to replace the silk robe with the shirt. The fabric was soft and smooth, even against their injuries. They slipped into the complementing arsenic waistcoat with tiny, delicate gold embroidery lines in patterns like shattered glass, sliding off the bed to replace their trousers with the matching arsenic green ones. Tao had even sourced a cravat. Nat turned back around, still tying an elegant knot at their throat.

Tao wasn't facing them. He had turned away to offer privacy as they changed. Something about the simple and understated offering, the way he had drawn no attention to the action, made Nat's shoulders a little lighter.

"How did you get these?" they asked, smoothing their hands down the front of the waistcoat, trailing fingers over the embroidery. The fabric was of the same type and quality as Tao's own, which meant they had to have been made in Shenai, probably custom made and, by the fact that they fit Nat perfectly, likely custom made for them specifically.

"I had a feeling I would see you again. I didn't want to be without appropriate offerings."

"When you say it like that, you make me sound like a magical being."

Tao turned and ran a soft hand down Nat's cheek. "Can hardly have a dandy out of their proper attire, can we?"

Heat rose in Nat's face under Tao's touch. The reassurance of being seen mixed with the mortification of the very same thing.

People didn't see Nat. They saw the glittery, shining exterior that Nat presented to the world and never looked deeper. And yet, here was this Pirate Lord that Nat had met only once before, who had gone out of his way to make clothes that would afford Nat the opportunity to wrap that glittery mask around themself once again. Which meant he had seen what was underneath that mask, recognised something about it the same way Nat had recognised the dandy in him, and he had offered a new mask despite that knowledge. Or maybe even because of it.

Nat watched him. Examined the perfect exterior he presented. Wondered which aspect was the key to unlocking what lay beneath. Would they ever be granted that access? Would Tao ask to be allowed under their own mask again another time? Or was this offering also the acknowledgement that it wasn't his place, that it should be Nat's decision as to who they showed that side of themself to?

Tao led them to the same room they had visited the last time they had been here, green velvet sofas with dark wood table beneath. Fresh fruit had been laid out on a platter along with bowls of rice and a generous portion of tea.

Tao took the same spot on the same sofa, so Nat sank down opposite him as they had the last time too.

This was nothing like any of the breakfasts they were used to, but they didn't let that stop them as soon as Tao had served the tea.

The pounding rain outside rattled against the roof. The only sound in the silence of the shared breakfast.

Tao picked up a slice of plum, his fingers trailing through his lips as he placed it in his mouth. Nat's eyes tracked the movement like a cat hunting.

They swallowed. "I have to ask," they finally said, shifting their gaze to the tea cup in their hands lest the visage of Tao disrupt their thoughts, or their confidence. "Me?"

"What about you?"

"You wanted..." '*We used to fuck'.* Nat could hardly say it in that manner. "Pleasure with me?"

"Of course."

He said it like it was the simplest thing in the world. Like anything else would be absurd. How could he see Nat like that? What appealed to him?

They squinted at him from under their hair. Wanting to see but not wanting to afford him the chance to see them in return. "Why?"

"Why what?"

"Why me?"

Tao's lips moved as if to start a sentence. A flippant, offhand comment. Something along the lines of 'why not?'— but he stopped before the words made sound, examining Nat as if it were the first time he had seen them. "Because you are intimidating and I like to play with dangerous things."

Nat snorted. Intimidating. Right, sure.

"And because you are a puzzle and I want to work you out."

"What do you do when you've finished working someone out?"

Tao's smile turned deadly. "Depends what I find underneath."

20
Look At Me, Dandy

This encounter was already dissimilar from the others. Not just for the conversations leading up to it. Most of Nat's experience had been centred in the location most easily and readily available and private — in whatever combination was there at the time. Which would have meant that very receiving room. The sofas looked plenty comfortable.

Instead, Tao took Nat by the hand and led them through yet another invisible door and into a room mostly filled by a four poster bed, dark wood twisted with shining gold that glinted in the lamps.

Nat almost wanted to ask, to tease Tao as to whether he had a secret bedroom off every other room in his house, but their throat was dry with nerves.

Tao tugged them in front of him. Behind him the door looked like a door, brass handle glinting in the light.

Nat's hand still in his, Tao crowded into their space, forcing them one step back. And then another. His mouth met Nat's once again. Insistent. Unquenching.

The world around Nat swirled as they fell backwards onto soft, green bed-sheets. The pain from their injuries protested but it mingled so well with the pleasure radiating out from their stomach. Riding the line of pleasure and pain.

Tao's hands pressed their wrists into the mattress beneath them, looming over with such presence that Nat could have claimed he filled the whole world.

Tucking one wrist under another left Tao a free hand to make short work of the buttons on Nat's waistcoat and shirt. Nat's body set to trembling. This was a whole different kind of exposed.

A swift tug at their cravat had the fabric unravelling into a heap beside their head. Warm fingers pushed the fabric aside. Nat let out an open mouthed gasp.

Tao's mouth shifted along their jaw, teeth scraping against their skin in a way that sent lighting sparking across Nat's fingertips.

"Leave your hands there," he whispered, hot breath washing over Nat's ear and sending their hips bucking.

His mouth travelled down, ghosting a line over Nat's recently exposed torso but not lingering long or focusing on much. His fingers came to rest on the edge of Nat's trousers and a wash of cold dread and fear froze Nat where they lay.

Tao stopped. Fingers ceasing all movement but remaining, softly, where they were. "What's wrong?"

Nat tipped their head back to look at their unbound but obediently static hands. When had they formed fists? They actively relaxed their hands, letting their fingers extend and curl to a comfortable point. The intensity of Tao's assessing gaze would be too much to cope with on top of fighting themself.

How could they begin to explain it? Quick fumbles in libraries held nothing to this already. And while Nat had been exposed in front of Tao before, it had held a different meaning than this. This was probably exactly why Tao had wanted a detailed conversation about Nat's experiences. It shamed Nat even further to know he had been right about it. That they had refuted the need for it.

"I... I don't want you to..." They squeezed their eyes shut. "Read something that doesn't exist from... what you encounter."

Tao shifted.

Nat closed their eyes. They had ruined it. Of course they had. They'd scared him off; just like everyone else they began to care about.

"Look at me, Dandy."

Nat forced their eyes open, forced themself to meet those endless dark depths of Tao's own.

"What I do or do not encounter during sex has no bearing on how I see the person. You, Nat, Dandy, are as you introduced yourself. Liege. Them. No matter what."

Awkward emotions tried to leak from Nat's eyes. They closed them again it, taking a deep, shuddering breath.

"Now," Tao said, tone turning dangerous and indulgent again as he leaned in to whisper in Nat's ear, "Be a good Dandy and keep your hands there for me."

Nat's almost sob turned into a moan as Tao shifted back down, pressing a solid kiss to their stomach before moving his attention back to their trousers. And then their thighs. And then his mouth refocused and Nat's hands flashed out to grab the headboard above them, to cling to something to keep them grounded, to keep them from spinning off into oblivion.

Tao's mouth had been menace enough when he used it to talk but now... this...

Nat clapped a hand over their mouth to stifle the unseemly noises that wanted to escape them only for a wrecked gasp to push through the futile barrier as Tao stopped.

"Now, Dandy." The playful disappointment in his voice had further heat coiling in Nat's belly. His fingers traced patterns on Nat's inner thighs, making them shift and writhe beneath him. "That's hardly being well behaved."

"I was never well behaved," Nat managed around panting breaths. "Should I have warned you?"

Tao chuckled, low and dark. "If you can't behave on your own, I may well have to find you a punishment."

The illicit thrill that sent through Nat was something they might have liked to investigate in their own time, alone and in private. But their body betrayed them arching up at the very idea and eliciting another low chuckle from Tao.

"Another time," he vowed. "This time..." he grabbed the cravat from beside Nat's head and wrapped it loosely around their wrists. No knot. Just a reminder, not a trap. Nat shivered.

"I want you to keep your wrists above your head."

21
You May Call Me What You Wish

"What is this?" Tao asked, fingers tracing the pattern of the swirling tattoo nestled below Nat's left elbow.

"You unfamiliar with tattoos, Princess?"

A smile twitched at the corner of his mouth. "That nickname is sticking, then?"

Nat shrugged and rolled to face him. "Is that okay?"

"You may call me what you wish, Dandy." He tapped the tattoo. "But this?"

"It's just a tattoo, why are you all so bothered by it?"

"All?"

"You, Aleksei."

"Pirates mostly get tattoos that mean something."

"It means something."

"Therein lies the question."

Nat rolled their eyes. "Pretty rich that you're grilling me on the meaning of my tattoo when you didn't even take off your shirt."

Tao held up his hands. "It was just innocent curiosity."

"I doubt anything you do counts as innocent," Nat teased.

Tao laughed and leaned in close to Nat's face. "I suppose that's a fair accusation."

Nat pressed their lips against his and let him pull them to straddle his hips. He slid his hands down Nat's torso, smooth even pressure that made them squirm above him. He gripped their hips, thumbs swiping, trailing, leading his hands further on their exploration.

Nat twisted their face away, hiding behind the curtain of their hair to avoid the intensity of his gaze. But they should have known better. Tao was in complete control here and he would have what he wanted. His fingers tugged Nat's face back.

Nat scrunched their eyes closed.

Tao ran his thumb over their lower lip. "You are shy."

"What can I say, it's my upbringing."

"Your well secreted upbringing." Even as he spoke in a conversational tone, the hand not on Nat's face continued its ministrations.

"I have made no secret of my upbringing," Nat said around the little gasps Tao's touches caused. "Just who did the job of it."

"Still unwilling to tell?"

"Like I told Aleksei, you can't addle me into it with touches and kisses." They opened their eyes, claiming the power in the interaction as they had so many times with other dandies. This situation somehow nothing and everything like those. "I've traded information around these activities since I was old enough to participate."

Tao's eyes flashed. Not the shame and regret of Aleksei upon the same kind of declaration. No, Tao's eyes flashed with greater interest, greater desire.

He wrapped the hand that had been resting on Nat's face around the back of their neck and flipped their positions on the bed, pinning Nat down once again.

"I knew you were dangerous," he breathed into their skin, words immediately followed by the brush of a hot, wet tongue up their throat. "Made all the clearer by the sea serpents swirling on your arm." His hands shifted, moving in such a way that had Nat throwing their head back. Tao's mouth gave chase, teeth digging tiny bites into Nat's ear. "You swirl around, Dandy, a cluster of sea-serpents all by yourself, able to drag people under if you so wish it. You are the most dangerous person I have ever brought in here. And you don't even realise the half of it."

Nat wanted to argue. Wanted to disagree. Wanted to throw the accusation, whispered like sweet nothings into their ear, right back at Tao. He was the Pirate Lord, far more powerful and dangerous that a nobody dandy with no links back to their family. Nat wasn't even a pirate. But the words disappeared in an aborted moan as the pleasure Tao had been teasing them towards dragged them under just like the sea-serpents he spoke of.

*N*at woke up as the door clicked. They jerked, yanking the blanket gently laid atop them closer around them, halfway to sitting before realising where they were and who was in the room with them.

Tao had frozen mid-step by the door. He set his foot down. "I didn't mean to wake you."

He was fully dressed again, not in the half-dressed state he had spent most of the morning with Nat. He was definitely hiding something under his shirt to be so steadfast about not just keeping it on but keeping it buttoned up his throat. Nat wasn't asking. A no was a no.

"Pirate Lord business?" they asked, shifting into a stretch, almost comfortable enough to release their blanket shield but not quite.

"Bustling port and a tropical storm," Tao confirmed. "And one ship complaining about a missing prisoner."

The relaxed comfort and lingering pleasure Nat had been enjoying turned bleak and sour. "That's it then?"

"What do you mean?"

"You're just going to hand me back again?"

"You think me so cruel?"

"You already did it once."

"That was different."

"How so?"

"It was before they did *that* to your back."

"I didn't think you a fool. Do you truly believe that was the worst of it?"

"I was trapped that first time. Grigg knew I had taken you, I leveraged my position as Pirate Lord to do it. When the Captain acquiesced to my demands I had little recourse—"

"Little recourse?" Nat snapped.

"And I *didn't* know."

"How did you think she treated her prisoners? Her walking cash?"

"I told you I never cared for ransom."

"You held me as one."

Tao coughed something that sounded like a shocked laugh. "You truly do think me cruel."

Nat offered a smile but it didn't feel comfortable, didn't feel like their typical dandy one. It felt mean and cruel and oh so much like the captain of *Poseidon's*. "You are the Pirate Lord."

They should have known better. Had known better. Should not have let themself get caught up in the relative safety, in the casual comfort of Tao's home. He'd already told them pleasure was enjoyed and then let go. They should never have come up here in the first place.

Why could Nat never trust themself to say no to a prospect? To something interestingly dangerous. The same impulse was always what got them in trouble. You'd think after this much time, Nat would have learnt their lesson. And yet. Here they were again. They had given themself over to someone else and they had been too much or not enough for that to matter.

They weren't clingy, could have taken pleasure with a defined end date, with no promise of continuation, no promise of a relationship. Even the notion of a relationship was almost laughable. But to be in his bed, in the aftermath, and with soft bruises from the way he had pressed his mouth and teeth into their skin, and to know that he wasn't only ending things but actively returning Nat to the dangerous thing he had all but saved them from?

"That almost sounds like an insult," Tao mused.

"Well, Peaches, I don't know what to tell you." They scrabbled for their discarded trousers, desperate for a barrier, for some semblance of modesty. Just because Tao had seen them completely laid bare didn't mean they had to stay that way, didn't mean he got to see it without Nat's consent.

"Peaches..." Tao echoed almost too quiet for Nat to hear. His lips thinned.

"Just give me enough time to find a different way out of port before you tell them? Do me that much?"

"Can I at least check your injuries?"

"You already did that this morning."

"Before we went through an... energetic experience."

Nat pressed their tongue against their teeth but let their shirt slide back off their shoulders to allow Tao access to their back and arm.

He unwrapped the bandages. "You got out of this well."

"If you say so." The words came out bitter.

"You're back is all bruised but it only broke skin in one spot."

It had seemed pretty bad at the time, but Nat supposed a lack of lingering damage was good, regardless of how it felt. "Are you some kind of doctor now?"

"Always have been."

Nat tried to look at him over their shoulder. "What?"

Tao smiled, wide and genuine. "Everyone is always so surprised to find that out. Do I not give off the aura of a doctor?"

"You're the Pirate Lord."

"And you are a dandy, high society, pirate."

"I'm not a pirate."

"Oh, my mistake. You're just a high society dandy who fucked the Pirate Lord."

Nat jerked the shirt back up their shoulders, separating Tao's hands from their skin. "Yeah, well, I've always been a slut."

Tao stepped away, throwing his hands up. "You have the most self-destructive streak I have ever witnessed."

"And what is that supposed to mean?"

"I mean you drag snark and sarcasm around you like a blanket. As if, if you hurt yourself enough nobody else can do it."

Nat steeled themself against the flinch. They had brought this on themself, challenging the first dandy they had come across in so long. Challenging the Pirate Lord.

"You pick up the flaws people lay at your feet, you catch the ones they toss at you like overripe fruit tossed at poor performers, and you stitch them together into your armour."

Finally dressed —bar their cravat, which had been lost somewhere in the bed— Nat fisted their hands at their sides. For the first time they regretted shirt sleeves that fit. Nothing to grip. Nothing to hide behind.

"It makes for poor armour, Nat," Tao continued, either oblivious to, uncaring of, or actively intended to create the hurt barrelling through Nat. Stabbing into their chest and surging up their throat to wet their eyes. "Armour should never have spikes on the inside. You need to forge yourself a weapon or you'll never survive this battle."

"What battle?" Nat asked their voice surprisingly even.

"Life."

22
So Mutiny, What's The Problem?

The rain had let up somewhat by the time Nat found the exit to the Pirate Lord's palace. That place was a maze. And, for some reason, none of Tao's people had appeared along any of the routes Nat had taken to find their way outside. It still came down in a relentless pour, but the clouds were fewer and further between, allowing a little ease of movement between pockets of rainfall. Allowing Nat to get to the main populated area of the Pirate Port admittedly soaked but not completely dishevelled.

Some of the stalls had reopened and the doors to the tavern Aleksei had snuck Nat to were slid wide, allowing full access to its interior. Nat slipped inside and slunk through the well placed tables and neatly tucked chairs to one of the booths lining the back wall. The seat was an uncushioned wooden bench —what was it with pirates and lack of comfort?— But the spot let Nat disappear into the shadows so they would take it.

Clouds rolled across the sky and the ships at the base of the hill where they rose and fell on the water. The storm faded further with every minute that passed. Nat needed a solid plan before it was truly gone and the ships began to sail out.

They searched their pockets for anything that might be tradeable. They expected to find nothing. What did they have? What had they had in their battered uniform trousers? Let alone what might have been transferred to Tao's gifted outfiture. But there was the pretty, if poorly embroidered ship on the fabric from the basket that hadn't seemed to be attached to anything else. It wasn't quite finished and Nat hardly expected anyone to want it. But it was nice that Tao had taken it from where Nat had pinned it to the sleeve of their destroyed shirt.

The server paused by the table. Nat held up the fabric. "Any chance you'd exchange that for a drink?"

She lifted the fabric and examined it, then offered Nat a soft smile. "You want tea?"

"That sounds wonderful."

It came in a tankard. Which was weird. But it was tea, black tea with milk and something sweet just the way it was served in Dinium. Nat held it close, nursing it as they tried to think of what they could do next. Should they just follow that original plan? Find a different ship and set sail for somewhere, anywhere, with the aim of eventually getting home? Would another ship even let them aboard with only sewing skills to offer? Especially since Nat had just traded away their only proof of skill.

"I'm just saying—" The words cut off sharply, as if interrupted but not by spoken words.

Nat looked up to find Jay, Bear, and Kajal the rigger wandering through the open doors.

Nat ducked further down in their booth as Bear signed, "You're always just saying!"

"He has a point, Jay," Kajal added. "If it's really a problem, why not take action?"

Jay threw xyr arms up. "What would you have me do? I'm not captain material and—Nat?"

"Nat?" Kajal repeated.

Jay pointed. "Nat."

Nat offered a shy wave and the trio of pirates invaded their booth. Bear's shoulders hunched.

"Hey, Lin," the rigger called. "Can we get our usual and another of whatever they're having?"

"You got money?" Lin asked.

Kajal laid some coins on the table's surface.

"What brings you to the tavern?" Jay asked Nat.

"Where else was I going to go?"

Bear's shoulders hunched further.

"If you have something to say, Bear, just say it," they snapped, emotions still uncomfortably pressed against the surface of their skin, as raw as the new wounds on their back.

"I'm sorry," he signed.

"For?"

His hands stalled, beginning and aborting several signs, searching for the right words.

"He picked you out," Kajal said.

"Kajal!" Jay cried. "Don't interrupt the man; we've only just learnt how to communicate with him."

"Picked me out?" Nat asked.

"As an expensive one," Bear replied. "Someone worth ransoming at all."

Nat sighed. "You didn't know me then. I'm not going to hold it against you. Any of you. I don't want to be that kind of person."

"Grudges are a waste of time," Kajal agreed.

Lin put the drinks on the table and slipped the coins into her apron pocket. "Sometimes they're useful."

Kajal stuck their tongue out at her.

Nat pulled the new tankard of tea toward themself. "So, what were you arguing about when you came in? What is Jay not taking action on?"

Hopefully the prompt would be enough to re-erupt the disagreements and let Nat sink back into their seat with the tankard.

Unfortunately, Jay took it as an opportunity to turn fully to Nat in the booth, lifting xyr leg up onto the seat to do so. "She never listens to any of us. We want things done certain ways and she just ignores us and does what she wants anyway."

"Who?"

"Captain."

Nat sighed. "Bear is right. If it bothers you all so much, why not do something about it? Aren't you supposed to vote in your captains?"

"Yeah."

"Doesn't that mean you could vote her out?"

"Sadly that's not how this works," Kajal sighed, sliding their tankard between their hands and making the liquid inside slosh.

"Why not?"

"Why not?" Jay echoed.

"Yeah. Why not? If you're all unhappy with the situation, just change it. You could leave and find new ships, start new lives, or oust her and stay where you are."

"You're suggesting a mutiny," Bear signed, seamlessly spelling out the word in a way that furthered Nat's opinion that he was once a well-educated young man.

Nat sipped their tea. "So mutiny. What's the problem?"

"It's not as simple as that. She's been Captain for years."

"Does that matter? Why would you choose to stay somewhere you're unhappy with?" Even as they spoke the words, Nat realised how easy it was to do just that. To stay in the situation you hated because it, at least, had the benefit of being known.

Before going to sea, Nat had never considered that life could mean anything other than their family home and society events. It wasn't about making change; it was about living through the situation and coming out the other side as unscathed as possible. Nat's whole life had been lived with the aim of coming out as unscathed as possible. They tucked their hand against their damaged left arm. It hurt in an entirely new way, a way that Nat hoped meant it was healing properly now that Tao had seen to it.

"We wouldn't know who to vote in as captain even if we did," Kajal muttered.

"Isn't that one of those 'cross that bridge when you come to it' kind of things?" Nat prompted.

"You can't have a ship without a captain."

"I'm not suggesting that you do. I'm suggesting you start working to find a captain who doesn't make you all quite this unhappy."

"All?" Bear asked.

"Isn't it? You three, Aleksei, the surgeon. Even Grigg doesn't like her."

Jay leaned forward. "Aleksei doesn't like her?"

"Are you kidding? Is that not obvious?"

"But he does everything she says."

"As do you." Nat waited, watching as realisation dawned on their three booth-mates. This was why it was vital to actually converse with other people, even if you did it in overtures and metaphors.

"Lin," Kajal called, dropping more coin on the table top. "We're gonna need another round."

23
Are You Going To Fight?

The new boarding plank rattled under Nat's feet as they strode up it. Their heart clattered around in their chest like an unsecured hat box inside an overturning carriage. The sword belt strapped across their torso hung heavy on their shoulder. Bear's sword, contained within, bumped their hip with each step.

They paused with both feet firmly on the deck of *Poseidon's Whatever*, the second word too worn by age and weather and the sea to make it out beyond it starting with an M. Mercy perhaps. Or maybe Myth. Not that it mattered.

The Captain's hat fluttered in the strong wind battering the ship toward the port, too strong to start thinking of leaving even if the deck hadn't still been slippery with rain. She stood in her usual spot at the bow of the ship, staring out over the sea. And beside her, as he so often was, stood Aleksei, facing toward the ship. Always her counterbalance as a good second should be.

Sucking in a breath, Nat took the stairs in one huge step.

"I didn't think you'd come back of your own volition," she said without turning.

"I was asked."

She snorted. "By whom? I know for a fact that my quartermaster hasn't been off the ship. Too busy sulking about what happened."

"I wasn't sulking," Aleksei argued.

"It doesn't matter who asked me," Nat said before the conversation could devolve. They only had so much ability to push past the way their lungs seemed to want to escape up their throat and out of their mouth. "It matters only why I'm here."

"And why is that?" the Captain asked.

"I'm here to tell you to leave."

She spun, hand flying to the sword at her hip.

If it got into that, Nat was done for. As much as Bear had insisted Nat bring a weapon, they had no foolish notion that they might manage to use it effectively against anyone let alone a well-practised swordswoman like this Captain. But Nat didn't have to fight. They just had to convince. So they smiled their perfect, practised smile. "I'm not going to fight you, Captain."

She hesitated.

Nat's dandified tone had morphed, taken on something of that alluring danger Tao displayed. Less frivolity, more innuendo. The implication that there was something under the words holding more weight, made more obvious and, by design, more threatening because of it. "I'm going to ask you nicely to vacate *my* ship."

"It's my ship!" she protested.

Nat laughed lightly, pressing delicate fingers to their collar where their cravat knot should have been. Except they had left that cravat in Tao's bed. Not thinking about that now. "Oh, Peaches. I don't think you understand. It's not your ship anymore. See," Nat strolled one way and then the other, desperate nervous energy leaking out of them in smooth, flowing motions. "You did what everyone always does. You underestimated the dandy. Dandies trade in information and I did what I do best:" They stopped, looking directly at her. "I got informed."

She blinked rapidly, trying to catch up, trying to piece together the information Nat was feeding her at their leisure. Building some kind of picture out of puzzle pieces she'd never had to use before. "What?"

Nat took up pacing again, fingers flying in motions, occasionally coming to steady the sword at their waist when it bumped slightly too hard. Did that come across as a threat? By the way the Captain kept flinching for her own swords, Nat was inclined to believe so. "I talked to the crew and they're not happy, they're not happy at all with the way you govern the ship. And the thing is, with pirates, democracy is very important. After all, Coded Pirates vote their captains in."

"How do you know that? How do you know about the Code?"

In truth, Nat knew nothing about the Code except what they had already said. It existed. It meant that pirates voted their captains in. And something about the Pirate Ports and the ship's quartermaster. It didn't matter, though, whether they actually knew anything. What mattered was whether they could convince this pirate Captain. What they could imply and insinuate. What they could make the Captain infer, what they could make her believe. "What did you think I was doing with the Pirate Lord?"

The Captain gave Nat a look that spoke volumes about what she thought Nat had been doing with the Pirate Lord. It would have been shameful, would have hurt someone else. Would have been damning in high society. Would have hurt someone like Nat if they *hadn't* actively and willingly participated in those same activities. But this wasn't high society. Nat wasn't someone else. And Nat wasn't going to let that bother them. They pulled their protective dandified personality tighter around themself, movements becoming more exaggerated, more foppish and absurd and incalculable.

"Oh, Captain," they sighed, affecting sympathy. "Can you not multitask? Not that it matters now. Your crew are unhappy, each thought they were the only one, or only one small group until I talked to them."

As more and more of them had trickled into the tavern, Kajal had called them to join the booth until they had needed to pull up another table, much to Lin's distaste. Nat's trio of booth-mates, though they had invited the crew into the booth, all tripped over their words too badly to be able to start asking the questions that needed to be asked. They were still afraid. Afraid that the others were perfectly content, that they would report back to the Captain and she would set out to punish Bear, Jay, and Kajal. Nat had seen her punishment now. Understood better why that fear clung so tightly to these pirates.

So Nat had asked. Not an outright 'Are you happy?' But softer, subtler questions. How did they feel about their duties? About ransoms? How did they think ships should be run? What was the deal with their Captain and the Pirate Lord? That one had hurt a little, what with Nat still nursing their wounded ego, wounded feelings and fickle heart.

And finally, Nat had asked each of the crew who joined the booth what they thought of the Captain's system of punishment.

"Now they— *we* want you off the ship." Nat gestured with a sweeping hand toward the boarding plank.

"You cannot, honestly believe I'll just leave because you say so, prissy little liegeling who won't even share their family name. I'm not giving my ship to a high society nobody!"

"I didn't ask you to."

The Captain smiled, thinking herself the winner of this argument.

Nat let her think it, stood wielding the silence just long enough for her smile to fade ever so slightly. They lowered their voice, mimicking Tao's dangerous register. "I told you to get off this ship because it's not yours anymore. Nobody said I was going to captain it instead. Coded pirates vote their captains in."

She turned to face Aleksei, stood at her right hand side as always. His eyes were blown wide, staring at Nat like they were some magical being, as if their words were as hypnotic as a siren's.

Nat laid a hand on the sword at their hip and stretched their other one out to him. "Sorry, Sunflower, but your choices are side with the crew or leave with her."

Aleksei took a step. Hesitated. "You talked to the entire crew?"

"Maybe not quite every single member, but yes."

"And they all feel this way?"

"Everyone I spoke to."

"This is absurd," the Captain snapped. "My crew is loyal. Aleksei is loyal."

Nat ignored her, refusing to look away from Aleksei's sparkling golden eyes. "You have to make your choice here. Decide where your loyalties truly lie. A single person? Or the crew you promised to provide for and protect?"

"I don't know if I can," he whispered.

Nat smiled softly. "We all make choices, even if we think we're choosing not to."

"Aleksei!" the Captain barked as he shifted over to visibly stand on Nat's side.

The wind swept over them, ruffling Nat's hair and making the rolled up sails clap. Nat smiled dangerously. "So, Peaches, are you going to fight?"

24
Pretend Pirate

Nat leaned over, catching themself on their thighs as they breathed shakily. After the Captain and her few truly loyal crewmates had left the ship, the remaining crew had gathered together on the main deck. Not relishing the thought of bumping into the recently ousted ex-captain in the port but having no stance amongst the crew, they'd dipped into the captain's cabin to collect themself.

She hadn't tried to fight in the end, which was good, because Nat didn't even know how to hold a sword properly. That would have been a very quick end to their career as a pretend pirate.

Now the crew would have a chance to vote in their new captain and would, hopefully, return Nat to somewhere near home in thanks for their efforts in ousting the ex-captain. It wasn't like they didn't know Nat was Endrish, between their accent, the other ransomed few, and that they were taken from an Endrish naval vessel. Still, closer to Dinium would be better. And Nat was hoping the crew would also leave them with enough cash in their pocket to barter further travel.

Someone knocked. Nat jerked to lean against the desk instead of their thighs and spun toward the door. Aiming for nonchalant, landing closer to tired.

Aleksei entered tentatively. "Found you."

"I wasn't hiding," Nat lied.

"Okay. Listen, we're really grateful—"

Nat's heart sank. Why couldn't they just learn their lesson? Pirates were not to be trusted.

"You want me to leave?" they supplied. At least it wasn't a demand for their family name so they could be successfully ransomed back. They would have to take the pitiful thanks of being left a free agent, even if it was shitty thanks for doing the scariest thing Nat had ever done in their entire life. Taking a pirate captain's ship away from her, staging a mutiny, threatening violence... "That's fine. I'll get out of your way."

Aleksei stepped in front of Nat, the door closing behind him, leaving the pair secluded. Alone. "No."

"No?" Nat frowned and then threw their hands up, stalking away from Aleksei and the door. What else were they going to do? Push past him onto deck where who-even-knew how many pirates stood? "Are you kidding me! You're going to try and ransom me back again, even though you still don't know my family name? Even though I just staged a mutiny for you!"

"Not exactly."

"Then what is it?"

"Part of the issue we had before you got here was that nobody wanted to be the captain."

Nat nodded.

"Nobody wanted to instigate the mutiny in case they got nominated to be captain."

"That makes a certain amount of sense."

"And, the thing is, that's still the case. None of us wants to be captain."

"I don't think I'd be much use in locating a quality pirate captain, Aleksei, dandy skills or not."

"That's not what we're asking." He took Nat's hands in his. "We're asking if, maybe, you might consider being our captain?"

"Me? I'm not even a pirate. I know fuck all about boats— ships— whatever. Why would you want me?" The same question they had asked Tao earlier that same day. Somehow it felt like forever ago.

"We don't need someone to run the ship. We can run the ship perfectly as we are. What we need is someone who will give us direction, someone who cares about each and every member of the crew. Someone who is entirely the opposite of *her*."

"But..." Nat had been intending to go home. Return to high society. That little box they had been built into.

"You don't have to agree. You don't even have to answer now. And if you don't want to, we'll take you wherever you want to go."

"Who voted for me?"

"It was unanimous."

Nat blinked. "You mean to tell me that every pirate on this ship wants me to be captain?"

Nat had never been good at following, never been included in a group because of it. Too independent for their own good, that was what everyone tended to say. And always too much for anyone to want to follow them. Except, apparently, these pirates. At least for now.

When Nat, inevitably became too much for them... well, like they'd said in the tavern, that was a bridge to cross when they got to it.

"Darling, Peaches, Sweet Pea." With each pretty nickname, the elegantly dressed pirate approached. The high winds tousled the bright red curls bouncing across their head, away from their sharp featured face. "I'm not sure what you've heard about dandies. I imagine you think dandies weak. And I certainly am the quintessential dandy."

They held no weapons, hands open as if ready to catch something out of thin air. Their shirt sleeves clung to their arms, too tight to logically allow for freedom of movement. The dynamic peacock patterned waistcoat hugged their torso, shining silk shifting with each breath. It shouldn't have made a threatening image.

Their face darkened. "But you could not pry this ship from my cold, dead hands."

The naval officer snorted, nostrils flaring with the noise. A Commodore, by the epaulettes on his uniform. The faded blue and dirtied white of his jacket sat a little ill, as if he had been at sea too long and some of his bulk had abandoned him.

"Just look at your crew." The dandy pirate gestured, stepping closer to the Commodore while he was distracted. Their nose wrinkled at the scent washing off him: perfume over the odour of an unwashed body. A smell too often found on naval officers. His brown hair stuck to his head with the grease of too long without a wash. "They're trying so desperately to subdue mine, but it won't work. Do you see?"

Below the pair of commanding officers, on the main deck of the pirate ship, clean and well-dressed pirates clashed in a chaotic maelstrom with dirty naval officers in ill-fitting too-worn uniforms.

"Fear," the dandy pirate captain whispered into the Commodore's ear. "Fear for what my crew could do when they fail. Fear for what you will subject them to if they live through that failure."

The Commodore's head snapped toward the dandy.

It made a certain level of twisted, naval sense that he had sought out the captain of the vessel. As if life ever made that kind of match. As if pirates worked like that. He probably just wanted the challenge of the strongest pirate available. Poor choice on his part. He'd have had more fun fighting Bear or Aleksei.

Still, the dandy pirate captain lifted his face with delicate fingers on his chin, forcing him to meet their hard eyes. "That's the big difference between you and me, Peaches–apart from your generally unwashed state. I cultivated my crew. I provide for their every need. And *I* was democratically voted in."

They smiled and stepped back. "But I know you're unlikely to be convinced by my simple words." They swung their arms wide, half invitation, half mockery of a bow. "Take your best shot. I won't even need a sword to defeat you."

Not The Pleasing Kind

Short Story

Tao's perspective of some of the events in Chapter 18 I Aim To Please.

ao pushed his dripping hair out of his face, the relentless downpour outside had tugged some of it from its usual plait, leaving the wet strands trailing in front of his eyes. From what he could see around the ruined shirt, Nat was hurt badly enough that they would need serious medical attention.

Bumping into them in his port in the middle of a storm had been a surprise – bumping into them the first time had been surprise enough but the middle of a storm was the least safe time to be out in the Shenai Pirate Port. Shenai bordered the Unknown World and storms were dangerous even without the risk of sea monster intervention. And the way Nat had been stumbling...

Now, inside his palace bathrooms with Nat sat on a jade bench in front of him, Tao pulled open the cupboard above their heads to access the medical supplies he always kept in here – as good a place as any, better than some thanks to the clean running water in here. Nat flinched from the flash of light on metal.

Tao swallowed. There was more to this set of injuries than just one of the many tantrums the Captain of *Poseidon's* was prone to. "I need to cut this shirt off," Tao explained, trying to keep his voice soft. It and Nat were both far too battered to take it off the way it was intended to be. Tugging fraying fabric over open wounds was always a risk at best and at worst painful and shock-inducing. Nat was already trembling.

Still, if Nat wanted to risk it to avoid a blade that was their choice to make. But they nodded their acquiescence leaving Tao to make short work of what was left of the containing pieces of shirt.

"I'm going to treat—" The words died in his mouth as the shirt fell away from not only Nat's obviously injured back but also their arms. A poorly wound bandage wrapped around Nat's left arm. It was just as drenched as everything else and, beyond that, stained from obvious reuse. An infection waiting to happen.

Why hadn't they asked him for new bandages when he had gifted them the now ruined shirt. But he knew, even without asking he knew. He wouldn't have admitted to the injury either.

Unwinding the bandages revealed lines of clean slices. Some of them overlapped with one another. Knife cuts that had intentionally been gouged into their arm. Judging by the way the skin beneath was swollen and pink, judging by the way the shallowest of them had begun to heal; these were part and parcel of Nat's piratical experience. Self-inflicted? No, the angle was wrong.

"Okay," Tao breathed, actively pushing aside his emotions before he could begin to categorise them. Nat didn't need a fuming Pirate Lord, they needed a doctor. "I'm going to treat your injuries. It might hurt but just..." He trailed off, completely unable to find the instruction needed, the comfort he wanted to offer. Tao had never been any good at comfort. His bedside manner was the number one thing people complained about; even as they walked away from situations they maybe shouldn't have been able to walk away from.

As Tao worked on Nat's injuries, he fell back into the habit of murmuring the instructions to himself, the way he had used to do with assistants, nurses, and interns. It had been called both comforting and disquieting, who knew which way Nat would take it. Who knew anything about Nat, really.

And then, Nat's voice slurred forth from their mouth, "Trees and birds."

Tao glanced up. Were they growing delusional? Hallucinating? But no, the paper screen in front of them was decorated with trees and birds, delicate deep green paint on almost white paper. Waxed to protect it from the dampness of the air.

Reassured that Nat was still coherent – at least mostly – Tao returned to cleaning the wounds.

"Is everything you own green and gold? Was it like that before you got here? Or did you change your clothes to match the building? It looks nice on you, don't mistake me, but I hope you like it." Their words cut off with a hiss of pain as Tao shifted to one of the deeper wounds, cleaning it until it began to, once again, sluggishly bleed.

"I shouldn't be talking," Nat babbled, beginning to sway badly enough that Tao had to catch and hold them by their uninjured arm. "I don't want to end up in trouble. I always end up in trouble. My own fault. I need to be more discrete. Not get caught sneaking into somebody else's library for a secret tryst with someone pretty."

Tao tried not to think too hard about that last comment as he finished his butterfly stitches on the deepest cut on Nat's arm. It wasn't infected, thankfully. He re-wrapped it to keep it safe and let go of Nat's shoulder, shifting to put the medical equipment away or into the appropriate place for it to be picked up and thrown away.

"It's one way to ruin a shirt," Nat offered into the silence, sounding more coherent.

Tao hummed, still unwilling or unable to find appropriate words to offer in the face of that. He should never have let them go back to that ship. He should have kept hold of them as his tribute. But he didn't want them to be stuck with him. That wasn't how Tao ran things. It was the awful legacy of his predecessor that Tao had already spent too much time trying to dismantle.

But letting *Poseidon's* Captain take back a prisoner who had once escaped was always going to have been a bad idea. She was known for her cruelty, for her skill walking the line of the Code, pushing at its boundaries but not quite breaking the rules.

"Couldn't help myself," Nat continued. "Desperate to see you again."

Tao swallowed thickly. There was a little too much sincerity there. Too genuine. Unprotected by the mask of foppishness that Nat usually employed. Or at least that Tao had seen them employ.

They wouldn't look at him. Whole body facing his but eyes dipped low, examining his hands. Were they looking for blood? His hands were clean.

"Had to get myself hurt to manage it."

Tao swallowed again. "You need to rest." His voice came out rough. An order. "Come."

"Bossy," Nat teased. "Just because you're a Lord doesn't mean you get to order me around."

Tao licked his lips. Oh no. bratty behaviour. Would they be that cheeky, that disobedience-adjacent in more intimate scenarios? If Tao gave them an order would they do it? Would they take that same teasing tone to call him bossy there too? Or, possibly more tantalisingly still, would they obey without question or comment?

Someone capable of teasing Tao like that and choosing not to.

But neither Nat nor Tao were in any fit state to explore such ideas. If Nat would even be interested in that with Tao anyway.

He slipped an arm around their waist to keep them from falling over on the way to the guest room.

They leaned in close, whispering in his ear in a haphazard fashion that sent their breath tickling under his shirt, tickling over his collarbones and the aged scar there. "You're not the only one with a title here, you know."

Tao swallowed again, closing his eyes for just a few steps over the carpet in the hallway. They were right. He wasn't the only one with a title. Nat hadn't been shy about confirming their stance as a Liege back in Enderand – though their Endrish origins had been extrapolated entirely by accent – just like they hadn't been shy about correcting Tao's presumption that Nat would have held to Endrish high society standards about purity and intimacy. But Nat had some level of experience and now... the idea that Tao might finally have found someone willing and able to play games of control back and forth... If they wanted to. Once they were healed. Once they had slept at the very least

Can't Wait To Hear More
From Nat And The Pirates?
Join The Mailing List At:
WillSoulsbyMcCreath.com
For exclusive and early access to
more of their stories.

About The Author

It's pronounced "Souls-Bee-Muh-Kreth"
As a cosplayer, Table-Top Gaming nerd, and videogamer; fiction has been a staple of Will's life forever. They like to corrupt their friends into joining these pass-times, or at least reading their stories.
Obsessed with every way to tell a story and every possible use for one, Will had few choices other than becoming a writer. A little too nosy for their own good they like to invest their time fixing other people's problems, and when that doesn't work they hand out stories to make you feel better.

Turn The Page For A Preview From The
Next Book

Not The Fainting Kind

1

I Will Bring You To Your Knees

There was something particular about partnered dancing which quartet or larger dancing managed to avoid. If one misjudged one's lead in a quartet or larger, it was easy to recover, for one's partner and for the quartet itself. The vast majority of the time, in a quartet or larger, mistakes became unnoticeable. With partnered dancing, however, a single wrong step had one careening into their partner. Most of the time that resulted in disaster. One particularly memorable case had included knocking a partner clear to the ground.

These days, Nat would be more likely to compare a quartet or larger to being like a well bonded ship's crew. Everyone moving in unison, clear on their own steps, and ready to step in to cover for one another's occasional missteps.

Nat's current position, however, was far more like partnered dancing. Facing someone one-on-one. Worse still, Nat definitely didn't know the steps and, certainly, should not have accepted the dance. Or egged on the naval commodore in question with a comment so boastful as not needing a sword of their own to defeat him.

The Commodore's sword rasped from its scabbard. The click of his heels meeting carried over the swoosh of the waves and the quieting sounds of the fight below.

Nat's heart demanded their attention, thumping heavily in their chest. What had they been thinking inviting him to fight? No. They knew what they had been thinking. That maybe, just maybe, their absurd over-confidence would be enough to put him off fighting all together.

Still. They were where they were.

Nat didn't even own a sword.

The Commodore thrust his sword toward them. Nat sidestepped the blade, feet moving in steps more practised in a very different scenario. The Commodore's feet, set shoulder width apart, moved. The front one stepping, the back one filling the gap.

"Are you seriously trying to fence with me? You can't fence a weaponless opponent, Peaches." Not to mention that wasn't a fencing sword. Who promoted this guy?

"You will not pick up a weapon with which to defend yourself," the Commodore snarled.

Nat presented their practised dandified smile. All ease and a little bit of snark. "I told you, I don't need one."

The next sword swipe held more aggression. With aggression came speed, leaving Nat reeling away from haphazard swings. The edge of the ship rapidly approached. Did he intend to push Nat overboard? As if any pirate captain worth their title wouldn't know ever millimetre of their ship with their eyes closed?

The blade glinted in the sun. Nat's eyes stung with the light. They swung an arm up to block their face. A burn of pain slashed across their forearm. Shit. The blade had caught them.

Still blinking away sunspots, Nat squinted as the Commodore whipped the blade at them once again. It came down as if to cleave their arm from their shoulder.

A tiny "Eep" escaped Nat, completely without their permission. They dashed to one side.

The sword lodged in the stern of the ship.

The Commodore yanked it. It didn't budge. He drew a dagger from his belt.

Nat didn't quite dodge fast enough. The blade cut into their waistcoat fabric, clanging against the boning that sat under the line of buttons down the front. It bounced out, bringing frayed silk with it.

"I will remove you from that high horse, deviant!" the Commodore snarled. "I will drag you to your knees."

They always seemed to think words like 'deviant' would hurt Nat's feelings. Always dove for them in the wake of a gentle prod like Peaches. Nat had heard worse. Nat had claimed worse.

On the Commodore's next jab, Nat spun around him, a move entirely drawn out of the popular dances from the last time they had been present in high society and been forced into dancing even though they never wanted to. They grabbed the man's shoulder and yanked his torso down into their rising knee.

The wind rushed from the Commodore's lungs. The knife in his hand clattered to the deck, skittering down the stairs to be lost in the chaos on the main deck.

Continuing their momentum, Nat grabbed the Commodore's wrist and yanked it behind his back. They whipped off the man's cravat – really? A simple slip knot? – and wrapped the fabric around the captured wrist.

They slammed their knee into his ribs again, further winding him so they could grab the other hand and secure it in the cravat-ropes. A harsh hand on his shoulders, they shoved him down onto the deck, whispering delicately into his ear, "What was that about knees?"

Acknowledgements

I think everyone who is gaining a mention in these acknowledgements knew a pirate book was on the horizon. Still, here we are.

Thanks to my mum for teaching me to read and all the other things. And for accidentally igniting my love of pirates with that wallpaper and that treehouse. Also, thanks for not being weird about the smut.

To my in-laws, for your endless joy in the next book and the next book and the next...

For my friends both online and irl. Jenny for introducing me to steampunk – I know this isn't quite that but Gaslamp and steampunk definitely impacted. Stew & James, and Jen for your wonderful, chaotic TTRPG adventures and all the ways that can chaotically fill time when stuck in one spot. Megan for still being my walking billboard. Avra, Sleepy, Sparrow & Orion, and my other Tumblr mutuals for your interest and your interesting stories.

To those who share their publishing experiences with the world for us to learn from and commiserate. I will never be anything but grateful for you all.

And, as always, the Pirate Queen herself, B, I cannot begin to thank you enough. Letting me talk endlessly, asking questions, formulating ideas with me that I then discarded. I can only imagine how strange it was to come home to find me dancing around my office/our living room in a pirate hat... at least the first time. Thank you for somehow being just as excited about this one as I was, I was relentless. Sorry and also you're welcome.

Thank You So Much For Picking
Up A Copy of
Not The Fighting Kind

For News About My Latest
Releases Sign Up To My Mailing
List At:
WillSoulsbyMcCreath.com

Or come find me on Social Media,
when I'm there I'm
@nopoodles

Enjoy my FREE Short Stories over
on
nopoodles.wordpress.com